MATING SEASON
A BEAR SHIFTER CAPTIVE ROMANCE

KITTY THOMAS

BURLESQUE PRESS

Mating Season

A BEAR SHIFTER CAPTIVE ROMANCE

KITTY THOMAS

Mating Season

Copyright © 2024 by Kitty Thomas

All rights reserved. This book may not be reproduced or transmitted in any form or by any means, except for brief quotations in reviews and articles, without the prior written permission of the author.

This book is a work of fiction. Names, characters, places, and incidents are products of the author's imagination or are used fictitiously. Any resemblance to actual events or persons, living or dead, is entirely coincidental.

Printed in the United States of America

Cover Art by Laura Hidalgo at Spellbinding Designs.

ISBN-13: 978-1-960480-69-9

Wholesale orders can be placed through the author.

Published by Burlesque Press

Contact the author at kittythomas.com Please use the "licensing" link in the top menu bar.

ACKNOWLEDGMENTS

Thank you to the following people:

Laura Hidalgo of Spellbinding Designs for the Mating Season Cover art

Lori Jackson for the teaser art.

The alpha team: Morgan and Lindsay.

Laura (a different Laura), for the book promo reels.

And my Pleasure House subscribers on Ream for their support: Ash J, Jill S, Sarah S, Emily H, Tish J, and Ashley.

1
ROSALIE

Stop me if you've heard this one... there's a hypothetical question that went around the internet that goes something like this: As a woman, would you rather be confronted with a bear in the woods, or a man? Every woman with a pulse says bear, to the absolute utter outrage of the entire internet male population.

They think we haven't understood the question. Or that we're just silly irrational women who don't get that bears are dangerous, or the damage a bear's claws can do. Maybe they think we have some Disney Princess fantasy where we sit in the forest singing while surrounded by all the woodland creatures. Maybe they think we think that bears can be our friends. I might think that last one just a little bit, but I'm not actually deluded enough to *really* believe it.

Who knows? I do know they think we're exaggerating the danger of the average human male stranger. Because their next flustered words are "Not all men!" Oh, that's comforting. Not *all* men. So as long as there's one shining unicorn white knight we should rest easy. I'm glad there was a man on the internet to explain this to me. You know if it was only a few men they'd say "Not most men", they'd never give up that opportunity for the moral high ground, but they give their game away because what they want... is access—easy access to their natural prey: women.

As far as I'm aware, I'm not a bear's natural prey. Fun fact about bears, they are hypo-carnivores which means they only get about thirty percent of their diet from meat. And even when hungry, a human isn't their first choice of food. They also aren't a territorial species. I'll take my chances with the bear. Thank you for your concern, random dude on the internet.

I'm actually hiking in the woods right now mentally obsessing about this stupid hypothetical question and how much it enrages me. By myself. At night.

Before you start your judgments about how foolish I am to be alone out in the woods at night, let me explain myself. And I'm sure actually the reason you're judging me right now is not because you thought I might run into a bear. Yeah. Exactly.

I was hiking in the middle of the day, and then I got lost, and then it got dark. That was actually a quicker explanation than I thought it was going to be.

I glimpse bits of the full moon through the spaces between the trees. An owl hoots in the distance because of course it does. And then I hear the crunch of leaves, and somehow I know that's a boot from a human... not the scurrying of an animal. It's too close, and contrary to many people's fears, wild animals don't tend to creep so close to humans for fun.

"You lost, sweetheart?" His voice is a thick southern

drawl. He's some good old boy that likes to be out in the woods. Is he hunting? Camping? Probably not hiking. Nobody really does that at night—except for me... who didn't understand the assignment... "be home before dark." Or at least safely locked inside your car.

"Um, no. No, I'm just fine," I say, backing away slowly and hoping he'll take the hint and go on his way.

I squint at the flashlight knowing it's too much to hope this might be a forest ranger and wondering if that would keep me safe or if the opportunity of discovering a woman out alone in the woods is just too much for far too many men who like to pretend to be protectors rather than the predators they often turn out to be.

No, I'm not bitter at all.

"Now, don't be like that..." he drawls. "You're clearly lost. Come back to my camp site... we'll get you fed and warmed up and then we can head out in the morning."

Who is *we*? Does he have others with him, or does he mean the *royal we*? Maybe he's fine. Maybe he's camping with people... men *and* women. If there are other women—couples—maybe it would be safe to go with him. But that prickle at the back of my neck tells me this guy did not come here with friends. And if he did, that only makes things worse—not better.

"No, I'm fine, really," I say. I take a few more steps back. He takes a few steps closer. I take a few steps back. He takes a few steps closer.

He knows exactly what he's doing as he shines the flashlight on me. It's a game to him, like a cat playing with a mouse before eating it. I can't see his face, but I can hear his smile when he says, "Don't you worry, I'll protect you from the bears."

I pull out my bear spray, but he bats it out of my hand.

His flashlight shining right in my face is doing me no favors for visibility of my situation. I take off my backpack and throw it at him, turn, and run.

My ID is in that bag. I really don't need him to have that bag, but I can't carry it and run at the same time, and the immediate problem is a stranger in the woods chasing me—not any future stalking worries. One problem at a time.

The only reason I can even see where I'm going is the flashlight he's shining in my direction as he chases me. The light wavers back and forth in front of my path matching the rhythm of his strides. He's not in great shape, but still, he'll catch me.

I try to think. I have no other weapons on me, the spray was it. My cell phone is in my pocket, but the last time I checked there was no reception out here. I pull it out anyway as I run and glance down... praying somehow I can get a couple of bars and call 911. Though I know they won't get to me in time, so what does it matter?

Tears cloud my vision. No bars—just like earlier when I first got lost. There were a lot of fallen leaves on the trail, and I took a wrong turn into what was actually the larger forest and not the continuation of the trail, and I haven't been able to find my way back to the path.

And all I'm doing is running deeper into a forest I don't know in the middle of the night with a mad man chasing me. What are the odds of that?

I trip over a tree root, and my cell phone goes flying out of my hand. A moment later he's on top of me. He flips me over as I struggle.

"Get the fuck off of me!"

"This doesn't have to be violent," he says.

The bile rises in my throat and I wonder if I can make

myself puke and if that will dissuade him off his course and kill the disgusting boner pressing through his pants against my thigh.

Doesn't have to be violent. This piece of shit. There are a million ways I wish I had the strength to overpower and kill this man.

I scream and squirm and manage to knee him in the groin. I roll back over onto my stomach to get up, but he grabs me by the ankle I sprained when my foot caught on the tree root. I howl in pain and try to kick him in the face with my uninjured foot, but he easily avoids the blow and drags me back to him.

"Please... you don't have to do this..." but I know I can't reason with a wild animal. And that's exactly what he is.

"Help!" I scream, as though there's anyone out here to hear me. And even if there were, how do I know it's not just someone else like this guy? They could make it a fucking party and multiply my trauma or maybe take a video for the internet.

No one is coming to save me. I reach through the leaves praying for a rock I can bash him over the head with, but nature provides me with no miracle weapon— not even a stick to jab in this monster's eye.

And then I hear it... a low growling sort of sound that turns into a roar. And then a second later the guy isn't on top of me anymore. I squint in the moonlight and can just make out... holy fuck it's an actual bear.

The bear is aggressive and angry. A grizzly maybe? Black bears are usually shy and far more scared of you than you are of them.

The man screams, and I realize this bear is attacking him full out. Like "Hiker gets mauled by bear" attacking. I scramble to get away, scanning the leaves for my phone. But I can't run on this ankle. *Fuck, fuck, fuck.*

Is the bear rabid? Will he maul me as soon as he's done with the man? The thought flits through my head that I'd prefer that death to what this man had planned for me.

The stranger's screams die, and I know it's because he has died. The bear turns back to me, his gaze seeming to glow golden in the moonlight.

I hear a male voice in my head that says, "Mine," as though I'm reading the bear's thoughts right out of his head. But of course bears don't think in English. I'm having some sort of break with reality.

I freeze. I can't think. I can't run. I just... freeze. And then I faint.

I don't expect to wake up. I expect to die like that man did.

But I do wake, in a cave, wrapped in a warm... bear? What the actual *fuck*? Is this bear... cuddling me? My back is pulled flush against his—or her, I don't really know—front, with an arm draped over me like this is normal.

Did this bear really drag me back to its cave...? It snores behind me, and I try to shimmy out from under the heavy furry arm. There's a grunting sound, and I'm gripped tighter.

Okay, Rosalie, at least you're alive. The bear didn't kill you. It's fine. It's... fine.

It is not fine. But the bear is too heavy and strong, and I am so tired. And my ankle is throbbing. I don't know if I could even get out of here on my own steam if I wanted to. I close my eyes and pray the bear doesn't wake up in the mood it was in when it mauled my attacker.

2

ROSALIE

Birds chirp just overhead, and the warm sun hits my face. I press back up against a very solid chest. There's a man's arm draped over me. I try desperately to climb out of the fog of sleep. Did I go home with a man I met at a bar? No, no bar. I went on a hike to clear my head and brainstorm a new painting.

And that's when it all comes flooding back. I barely breathe. There is a man with his arm wrapped around me, but it can't be the man the bear mauled. I saw him die. Didn't I?

I try to calm my breathing and slip out from underneath the strong tattooed arm.

"Where do you think you're going?" It's a low, guttural voice. Definitely not the man from last night.

I don't want to say... sexy. Objectively it is sexy, but after what almost happened last night, the last thing I need to be thinking is a thought like that in a situation like this.

"Let me go," I ground out. Maybe it's the daylight

making me braver, or the stupidity of being attracted to that masculine gravelly voice—like maybe I wouldn't want to resist if he decided he wanted to... *Stop that thought right there!* I've never gone to therapy in my life, and clearly that was my first mistake.

He loosens his grip, and I jump out of his arms like I'm on fire. I turn and my eyes widen. He's naked. I should run right now, but I can't. I'm still hurt. The pain slices through my ankle, and I take the weight off it, trying not to let him see my injury. As if I could outrun this man anyway.

"W-what happened to the bear?" Did I hallucinate that? There was definitely a bear. But how could this guy take out a bear without me even waking up?

"Just calm down, Rosalie, I'm not going to hurt you."

"H-how do you know my name?"

His head tilts to one corner where I see my bag and cell phone. And weirdly, the bear spray.

"I'm the bear," he says calmly.

I just stare at him. I mean I *really* stare at him... those tightly coiled muscles, washboard abs, sun-kissed skin, tousled dark hair, warm brown eyes with flecks of amber, strong jaw, a very neat short beard a couple of steps above a five o'clock shadow—not too mountain man—tribal tattoos running around his arms and over his chest... a happy trail that leads down to... *look up, look up!*

I shake my head out of this madness.

He just smirks. He's one of those guys who knows exactly how hot he is.

"I'm sorry... what?" I could swear while I was ogling him, he said he was the bear, which is crazy so obviously I'm dreaming, or dead, or hit my head, or randomly developed a complex delusional disorder. Who really can say?

"Rosalie, I'm the bear."

"What?" I say again. My brain refuses to compute this. Okay so he's the crazy one. Yay for *my* sanity. But that doesn't explain how the fuck he got the bear out of here.

"You are not a bear. What did you do to the bear?" I say.

"Look around."

I do, this time really taking in my surroundings. The sunlight that was shining down on my face... in a cave... is explained by the hole in the... ceiling? There's a fire pit right under that hole for air flow from cooking. There are bear skin rugs all over the cave floor. He kindly drapes one of them over his dick. Too little, too late, there buddy. There's a cabinet with drawers on one side.

"Do you think I somehow killed a bear and built some cabinets in the middle of the night without you waking up?"

I shake my head. "You cannot be a bear. That's not real."

He sighs. "I guess you'll see tonight. Until then, I'll let you believe what you want."

I laugh, "I'm not going to be here tonight."

I slip my cell phone and bear spray back into my pocket and put on the backpack, trying not to wince from my ankle.

I limp out of the cave, not knowing what direction I'm going in. I am still lost, after all. A few minutes later, the man who seems to think he's an actual *bear*, is following me. He has kindly put on some jeans.

I mean, I understand that cave I slept in is clearly a human dwelling. And yet the bear dragged me right into it... unless I dreamed that last bear part. How do I know I even woke up in the night? Maybe that part was a dream.

Yes! That's what happened. Maybe after I fainted, this guy who also just happened to be in the woods nearby, somehow killed the bear and got my stuff and took me back to his... person cave where he sleeps naked in the fall. Sure, that sounds way better.

I flinch when he grabs my arm. "Rosalie, you're injured. And I can't let you go, anyway."

I swallow the lump quickly forming in my throat. I mean, yeah, sure, he's hot and all, but also clearly troubled.

"Look, I appreciate whatever you did to save me from that bear that was clearly going to kill me after he killed my would-be rapist, but please... I really have to go."

He sighs. "I'm sorry but I think you're my mate, so letting you go would be quite impossible at this point."

I just slow blink at him. "Do you mean mate like Australian friend?"

"No. I mean mate like... Fated Mate."

Okay, someone has been watching some teen paranormal TV dramas. Hey, no judgement. I just laugh at him because really what else can I do?

"Just wait, you'll see tonight. I'm a bear. It's the third and final night of the full moon, then we can go back to my place in the city and get you moved in."

"What? No, I'm not living with you. I don't *know* you." Yes, let's just move in with the mentally ill forest man who thinks he's a bear. What could possibly go wrong?

"I'm Cooper."

"Great. I'm leaving." I try to hobble a little further, but he swoops me up in his arms and carries me back to the cave.

"Hey! Put me down!"

He does put me down—on a small chair next to a table inside the cave.

"I really don't want to tie you up, Rosalie. You cannot leave. You are mine, and I can't let you go until the mating is complete."

I feel the tears gathering in my eyes. "You are legitimately delusional, and that scares me a lot." There's no point in putting on a brave face. I'm in the middle of nowhere and injured. Maybe I can find a way to break through his delusion and save myself.

He kneels beside my chair and brushes the back of his warm hand over my cheek. I do *not* lean into it like some pathetic damsel.

"Shhhh, please don't cry."

"Then let me go," I whisper.

"No. I absolutely cannot do that."

"You mean won't, not can't. You're not a bear, Cooper, just another piece of shit human male who feels entitled to fuck. You're no better than the guy last night. Just a prettier monster."

It takes everything in me not to let my gaze rove over the evidence of all his prettiness.

His features go dark, and his jaw clenches. "I'm not going to rape you, for fuck's sake."

"Well, you just assumed I'd fuck you and said you can't let me go until I do, so... I genuinely don't get why you don't get that sounds like rape to me."

He stands up and takes a few steps back, then he does this motion with his hands like he's showcasing a brand new refrigerator on a game show, except he's the refrigerator.

"Really? You don't want all this?" He waggles his eyebrows suggestively at me.

Oh my god. Could he be any more arrogant right now? *He's not wrong*, my traitorous brain supplies.

"You *are* straight, right?" he prods.

"That's not the point."

"Well, I know you don't have a husband or boyfriend."

I cross my arms over my chest, my anger starting to edge out my fear. I wonder if he's pissing me off on purpose so I'll stop crying. "And how would you know that?"

"I only smell the man from last night on you. So unless you're with a long haul trucker or a soldier that's currently fighting a foreign war, you're single."

"So? Maybe I *want* to be single. Did you ever think of that? Maybe I have no interest in having my life revolve around a man. There's way more shit to do in this world besides half-assed romance. And trust me, most men can barely half ass it."

"Fate has a different plan, I'm afraid." He doesn't say anything else, just gets up and goes to the cabinet. I don't bother trying to escape... it's pointless with this ankle, and we both know it.

3
COOPER

Last night. Before it happened.

I don't really like to hunt as a bear. The wolf shifters seem to like it a lot but the only thing worth hunting in this forest is rabbit, and it's too gamey to me. Usually I do what most bears do... find human junk food.

There's a gas station about five miles away where I like to get free snacks. Yes, as a bear. I just walk right in. The owners think it's hilarious—a bear in their little food market aisle with a favorite snack. I get Gummy Bears a lot just to mess with them. And Snickers' bars.

Shifters have a high metabolism but I'm also pretty dedicated to my physique. Anything a shifter eats in their animal form has no direct caloric effect on their human form, so I tend to eat most of my cheat meals on the nights of the full moon.

Tonight I just sit in the middle of the aisle and gorge on chocolate. They think I'm the smartest bear in the world because I've "figured out" how to get the wrapper off. I just slit the plastic with my claw and push out the candy. Bears aren't really supposed to have chocolate, but as a shifter I have neither the normal frailties and illnesses of a human or of a bear.

When I'm finished with my petty crime, I begin to amble out the same way I came in. I get that it's a little shitty for me to steal from a gas station every month, but it's really less about getting away with the theft and more the thrill of them thinking I'm just a bear, all the while I know the truth... that I can understand every word that comes out of their mouths.

And anyway... I'd hardly call it stealing. Brenda and Bob Bronson—the couple that owns this fine establishment—started a Youtube channel that now has over a million subscribers. They film all my antics. I'm internet famous, and what they make in ad revenue more than makes up for what I steal every month.

I take a bag of BBQ chips for the road and then I head back to my den in the forest to sleep off my junk food bender. I'm about half a mile from the den when I hear a woman cry out. "Help!"

Does she think there's help in these woods? She's not far from me. Is it an animal threat? Another human? I decide to investigate. When I get closer I see it's a human male, and then something in me just... snaps. I make angry chuffing sounds and then I roar... something I don't typically do as a bear.

Then I charge that motherfucker and use the full force of my seven hundred pound weight to send him sailing. He lands several yards away, his back hitting a tree, and I could swear I heard it crack. He's screaming and trying to scramble away.

"Yeah, how does it feel, motherfucker...to be the prey for once?" But of course human speech doesn't come out of my mouth, only bear chuffs. But I know what I said. I smell the acrid aroma of urine as he full on pisses himself.

And then, without hesitation or a single moral quandary, I maul him to death.

I don't normally maul humans, but this guy has me pissed off. And I don't really know why until he's dead and I've made my way back over to her. Her terrified eyes meet mine, and then she faints.

I want to follow her down the dark path to sweet oblivion because I've just realized why I lost my chill and killed that guy. This girl is mine. My mate. And I cannot let another living male touch her ever the fuck again.

4
COOPER

N*ow.*

She thinks I'm delusional, and she probably wouldn't be that wrong but for far different reasons than she thinks. This is the first time I've ever had a woman in my den. Oh, I've had them in my penthouse in the city. I'm not a monk. But I've always known those could only be one night stands and short flings at best.

I can't do that to a woman... let her fall in love with me and then throw her away because fate decided to give me my mate at an inopportune time. A shifter could be married with four kids and deliriously happy, but if they were foolish enough to choose their own partner and then their true mate showed up, that relationship they thought was so special, is over.

I've seen decades-long loves end, all because that

bitch fate decided to fuck around with some lives. So, like smart shifters, I have remained a bachelor and never let any woman get too close to me—mostly, anyway. Anyone who isn't your true mate is for playtime only.

And here she is, a gorgeous petite brunette with shimmering green eyes, all for me.

I'm only thirty. Often it's decades before a shifter finds their mate. In a lot of ways I'm lucky... and in a lot of ways I'm not.

A mate can be another shifter or a human, and I was hoping against all hope it would be another shifter because shifters understand this. They accept this. A human does not. Rosalie cannot understand how impossible it would be for me to let her go. I just rescued her from a fucking rapist in the woods, and I absolutely know how this looks to her. But until the mate bond is complete, she won't understand... can't understand.

I really hope I don't have to become a monster to secure this union because the thoughts running through my mind... the needs... And I don't just mean sexual. There is a clawing need for her to be here with me, for her to never leave my sight... at least until the bond is complete. Then I won't have to worry as much. I'll know where she is, what she's feeling, if she's in danger. At all times.

But right now? She's fragile. *This* is fragile. I could have lost her last night. If I'd been just a little bit later would my mate be dead in the woods right now? All because I ate just one too many candy bars to entertain random viewers on the internet?

Would fate send me another or would I just ignorantly wander the earth for centuries thinking she was coming when I'd already failed her?

"If you're a bear, why do you have bear skin rugs in

here? That seems a little psychotic don't you think? It would be like if I had a people-skin wallet in my bag."

I sigh. I'm sitting on the floor next to her chair, inspecting her swollen ankle. I wish I could have done something about it last night, but... bear. While older shifters can shift at will, most of us can only do partial shifts until the three nights of the full moon where we must shift and don't return to human form until morning.

I was wide awake most of the night counting down the time until I could shift back and look at that injury and really tend to it properly.

"Can you wiggle your toes for me?"

"Foot fetish?" she asks, the snark in her tone as sharp as a razor blade. She's cute as fuck, but that mouth... that mouth is going to get her into some trouble.

"I just want to make sure it's not broken and see the extent of your injuries. As for the rugs, those are my ancestors."

"Oh, that makes you sound well-adjusted and safe to be around," she says.

This is going to be a long day. "Shifters live a long time. Centuries. We age much more slowly than humans. We also don't have the kind of rabbit-like fertility humans have. When one of us dies, part of our rituals to honor the dead involves preserving the... hide and passing it down. It's a way in which the ancestors are always with us."

"What if they die as a human?"

"They won't. Shifters always shift before they die. Now wiggle your toes."

She does, reluctantly, and I'm relieved at least it isn't broken. I stand and take her hands in mine to help her up.

"Now try to put some weight on it."

She does and grimaces against the pain.

"Can you walk on it at all?" I know she was walking, sort of, not that long ago, but if she lets it tighten up she could lose that ability quickly.

She half hobbles around the den, but it's something at least. I had a human friend who once sprained his ankle so badly he couldn't walk without crutches for three months. This is decidedly less serious. I help her back to the chair.

I proceed to rub a healing salve that has been in my family for generations onto her ankle. Shifters usually heal instantly, but there are wounds made with silver weapons that require first aid.

It isn't true that a silver bullet or weapon will necessarily kill us merely because it's silver. It just slows our healing to that of a human. An injury that would be instantly fatal to a human is only fatal to us with silver. And an injury that wouldn't kill a human, won't kill a shifter either—even if silver is used. Even after a bullet is removed, the exposure to the silver has a lasting effect. So, I keep a first aid kit everywhere—just in case.

I've never been grateful for this shifter weakness, but without it, I wouldn't have anything to tend to Rosalie's injury right now.

"That smells rank," she says.

"That's how you know it's working." I massage the salve in and try not to develop a foot fetish. Then I wrap her ankle, grateful I keep such an extensive first aid kit.

"Well, I can't be your mate, because that would be tragic."

"How so?" Maybe she isn't attracted to me. I'm well aware of my charms and the effects I have on women, but maybe I'm not her type?

"Humans don't live for centuries. Why would you want a human mate when I'm just going to age and die much sooner than you? I mean... sure I'm twenty-five now, but in a couple of decades I'll start to get wrinkles and gray hair and then start falling apart while you continue to look like this..." she gestures at my body.

I know she's just humoring me, playing devil's advocate. Everything in her tone tells me she thinks I belong in a mental ward. So since she already thinks that... I may as well keep dropping facts about my world on her.

"My bite will take care of your aging problem," I say.

Her expression closes off and she jerks her foot out of my hand. "You're fucking crazy, and I want to go home."

Nightfall can't get here fast enough. I get up and go through the cabinets and pull out some protein bars and bottled water and place it on the table next to her. "This is all I have right now, but as soon as the sun goes down and I shift, I'll go hunt for us."

And by hunt, I mean steal some packaged deli sandwiches from the gas station. Bob and Brenda will be amused by my new "healthy diet".

She eyes me warily but opens the water and one of the protein bars. "What about you?" She's regrouping and seems to be going for appeasement now, though I doubt it will last long with her sharp tongue.

"I ate plenty last night. I'm good for a while." I'm used to intermittent fasting, but I don't tell her that. The bear thing is probably enough for now. She doesn't need to know about my psycho diet and workout regimen.

"Did you eat my attacker?" she asks conversationally. And at this point I'm not sure if she's starting to believe me a little or if it's still part of her sarcastic cross-examination.

"Gross. I don't eat humans, Rosalie."

"But you keep your ancestors' skins. I'm sorry, but it's

difficult for me to keep up with the ins and outs of your magic world."

I roll my eyes. I highly doubt it's difficult for this woman to keep up with anything.

But she's not done. "So, tomorrow when you're a real boy again, where exactly are you taking me?"

Yep, she is definitely not on board with any of this. She's trying to get information to plan her escape. No doubt she's heard all the warnings about your kidnapper taking you to a second location. Though technically wouldn't my den be the second location?

I can't really blame her. Even with her being my mate, I'd probably lose some of my attraction if she was just going to take my word for all of this and follow me around like a lost star-eyed puppy.

"My penthouse in the city," I say.

"Oh, so you're a *rich* werebear? How nice for me."

"Don't call me a werebear. I am a bear shifter. And yes, I'm rich. Old money. It isn't just vampires who can use the wisdom of time and compound interest."

I'm really not sure why the stereotype is that all vampires are rich and all shifters are living simple humble lives out in the woods. Being a bear doesn't make me like a penthouse view any less.

She snorts. "Vampires are real, too?"

"Yes."

"Of course they are."

She rolls her eyes, but her sarcasm is starting to give way again to fear. There is nothing that will convince her I'm telling the truth short of a live demonstration.

We spend the rest of the day in mostly boredom and uncomfortable silence. I can think of a million things I'd like to do with her right now that would definitely fill up the time until my final shift this month, but I know there's no way she'd go for it. She needs to see the truth first, and then we'll go from there.

Finally night comes. The painful snapping and cracking and rearranging of bones and organs commences as the moon rises higher into the sky. I strip off my jeans before the change can fully take me and fall to the ground, my hands reflexively clenching and digging into the dirt. I'm sure this isn't the most attractive thing for Rosalie to have to witness, but she has to know. Once she sees the truth, maybe it will be easier to reason with her and make her understand.

We've spent the entire day with her thinking I'm delusional. When she sees the change, I can at least eliminate that objection to our union.

When the shift is complete and the pain recedes, I turn to Rosalie who looks on me in absolute horror. It's worse than the way she looked at me last night, before she knew there was a person in here. I raise my hands in the placating way humans do, and then realize belatedly that a seven hundred pound bear raising his arms in the air isn't taken in exactly the same way as when I do it in my human form.

She screams and cringes away from me, and I quickly go back to my former stance. I can't communicate with her like this, so I fight every instinct inside me and leave her alone in the den to go get us some food. She can't get far on that ankle, and while the mating bond may not be completed yet, I still have the senses of a bear and can easily track her in this forest. If she tries to leave, she won't get far.

5
ROSALIE

Holy shit, Cooper is a fucking *bear*! My knuckles are white from where I just gripped the chair. I've gone back and forth all day over whether he had a legitimate delusion or if it was some kind of extended joke that just wasn't funny.

I almost laughed when it got dark outside and he started making these pained sounds and contorting in all kinds of weird positions. I was about to say, "Ha, ha, jokes over. You got me." when his body parts started to actually *change*.

At first it was a ripple, almost like his skin was a blanket that a small animal was crawling around underneath. And then fur started to sprout. There were awful cracking sounds and groans of genuine pain. His eyes glowed. Claws extended, teeth lengthened into fangs, and a few minutes later, he was a fucking bear!

He reared up on his hind legs and for a moment I thought he was going to attack me, so I screamed. Then he left the cave—maybe to hunt like he said he'd do earlier.

Shit. Shit. Shit.

My brain is stuck on a loop right now. He was serious. And... plot twist... not crazy. The entire day I've been stuck with this guy trying to manage and appease his possible mental illness, not once did I really think he was an actual bear. I guess that thing last night with him cuddling with me wasn't a dream after all. Clearly I'm the delusional one here—or just in deep denial.

As soon as I process all of this, the truth of my reality comes crashing into me. He thinks I'm his mate. He plans to bite me. He plans to keep me his captive until and unless I let him *bite* me... and turn me into a bear like him?

No. I can't. I don't want to be a bear! I can't handle what he just went through. I definitely can't do it three nights a month for... centuries. No. Fucking no. I have to get away from this guy right now!

I wince as I struggle to a standing position. I've been trying to rotate my ankle, to keep it moving throughout the day, but it still hurts like hell when I stand up. Pins and needles shoot through me. And even so, I know that this pain is nothing like what the change into his animal form causes. Cooper is the one guy who actually might be able to understand the pain of childbirth. But women don't give birth three times a month for the rest of their lives! Nope. I am out!

I cannot let him bite me. I can't let him make me a bear. I feel unhinged just thinking these thoughts. And *vampires* are real, too? Jesus. What the fuck is this reality? How have I gone my whole life not knowing any of this existed?

As I move around the cave I'm relieved that actually I think my ankle is a bit better. Maybe that stinky salve really does work. I pick up my cell phone, praying to get reception.

But, no. Of course not. Why would I need to call anybody out in the middle of the woods! Maybe I can take it and go outside... maybe there's a patchy signal somewhere. But he'll be back. How long does it take to hunt? Probably not that long.

I'm pretty sure he's not going to bite me tonight as a bear, but when? How long is he going to give me before he does this? And not only that, he intends to tie me to him for life. What if I wanted to be single? Serious question. What if I wanted my own house and a hoard of cats and just to be left alone!

I have goals. I have shit to do. I do not have the desire to be some bear shifter's life mate. Oh my god, am I going to give birth to a bear cub? Why did I have to twist my fucking ankle? It's such a cliché. It's always the ankle.

I start going through cabinets and drawers not even knowing what I'm looking for. Maybe a weapon? I probably can't do much to him tonight in this form, but maybe when he's human again? I mean I have the bear spray but I doubt that would be as useful on him as it would a normal bear. Still, I could try.

Even if I do find a suitable weapon, I'm not sure I can bring myself to kill him, especially not after he saved my life last night. But if I can find a way to incapacitate him, maybe I can escape. Because I'm sure once he gets me to his actual normal home, he's going to have a much better way to keep me prisoner, and I'm going to have much fewer opportunities to escape.

And now I'm crying with relief because I just found a satellite phone, and it has juice. He must have brought it up with him in case *he* needed to call someone out in the middle of the woods.

"911, what's your emergency?"

"Hi, I'm lost out in the Cherokee National Forest. I've got an ankle injury, and I need help."

"Are you bleeding, Ma'am?"

"No, it's just a sprain."

"Keep your phone on. We are tracking your coordinates."

I grab my bag and slip my useless cell phone and the bear spray back into my pocket and then limp out into the night.

I move slowly through the trees, trying to find a more open spot. They'll be sending a search and rescue helicopter probably, and I want them to be able to see and get to me easily—especially since Cooper could return at any time.

Half an hour later I hear the whir of the blades and see the giant spotlight. I wave my hands back and forth at them to make sure they see me.

"Just stay where you are, we're coming to get you," a voice says out of a megaphone.

Oh thank god.

But then I hear a soft growl. I turn and there he is. And he's got... wrapped deli sandwiches in his mouth. I thought he was going to hunt, like... a rabbit or a deer or something.

"Cooper, please. Just let me go. You can't take me now. They've already spotted me. If you drag me off they'll chase you, too. You think they don't have tranquilizer guns? You think they aren't prepared to deal with wildlife out here? And what if they find out what you really are? I won't tell anyone, I promise, if you just let me go."

Who would believe me anyway?

He drops the sandwiches on the ground and chuffs softly back at me. I could swear he's trying to talk... like he's trying to reason with me. He takes a few steps forward, and I hold up a hand. "Stop! No! Let me go! This will not end well for you if you try anything. Accept defeat. They'll take you out with a tranq gun and I'll tell them what you are myself, I swear to fuck I will. I'll do whatever I have to do. Don't put me in survival mode, Cooper. Just... don't."

He sees the people getting closer to me, and he knows I'm right. He looks... hurt. I am not going to feel sorry for a man who wants to keep me his prisoner and doesn't give a shit about what I want.

He growls again and then finally backs away into the shadows of the forest, and I let out the breath I didn't know I was holding.

6

COOPER

She's right. As much as it kills me, the smartest move is to hang back and wait, wait for a moment with no witnesses, wait until I have my human form back.

I'm so fucking stupid, why didn't I remember I brought the SAT phone? Why? *She can't get too far on that ankle.* I was so foolishly confident.

I chase the helicopter. I'm sure with her injury and being lost in the woods for an extended time, they're taking her to the hospital to check her out, but still, I can't stand to let that helicopter leave my sight. Why couldn't I have had a shifter mate?

Most shifters would have accepted me without question or struggle. I've been to more than my fair share of Find Your Mate mixers where we hope to nudge fate a little. At every single one of those events, any of the female shifters in attendance would have been thrilled if I was their match.

But no, it just had to be a human. I remember Rosalie's

address from her driver's license. Maybe it would be better to wait at her apartment, but I can't bring myself to do that. Instead I chase the helicopter all the way to the hospital.

The nearest hospital is only about five miles from the edges of the forest and still outside the city limits—plenty of wooded areas to hide in around the parking lot. But of course I don't do anything so smart as that. I wait near a dumpster, trying to ignore the smell of a half-eaten cheeseburger someone threw out.

Keep it together, Cooper. I'm not about to dumpster dive to stress eat.

The wait is long. I pace out in the parking lot, watching her sitting in the waiting room. She's not in an official emergency but I'm glad she'll get an X-ray and a real doctor visit. Technically even with the toe wiggling, she could have a hairline fracture, and it's just better to get it checked out.

When they finally take her back I prowl around the hospital, sniffing at all the windows until I find the room they're seeing her in. The clock on the wall says it's only ten o'clock. Fuck, I need my human form back right now. I can't do shit as a bear—not useful shit anyway. The sun won't be up for nine hours.

After another hour, they put her in a boot and release her to her roommate who came to pick her up. I can't directly chase the car so I take back roads to beat her to her place. I narrowly escape being spotted in the parking lot by the headlights of her roommate's car.

Her apartment is on the third floor of her building. I clumsily climb the fire escape to get to it. She doesn't realize her window is open a crack, and either way I doubt she'd consider a bear could get up here. Even normal bears are surprisingly dexterous and resourceful—especially when properly motivated. And I am definitely motivated. My mate is in there.

"I don't understand this," her roommate says.

"I have to get out of here, Nikki."

"But why? You're not making any sense. You said there was a man in the woods? Just call the police. Get a restraining order."

"He knows where I live. And how many women get restraining orders and die for their trouble?"

She's walking much better with the boot as she throws clothes into a suitcase. I watch the screen light up when she opens her laptop.

"What are you doing now?" Nikki asks.

"Booking a last minute flight. I need to get out of here tonight."

"No, what you need to do is sleep."

Rosalie shakes her head and types quickly to pull up a site for airline tickets. "I'll take a red eye and sleep on the plane. I'm going to have to use my savings and fly first class though, so I can elevate my ankle." She types and scrolls. "Dammit, If I want first class, there's a layover in Phoenix."

"Won't it be safer to go during the day?" Nikki says.

"No."

I wish she didn't have a roommate. I could so easily get into this apartment and corner her until morning. But I can't do it now, not with a witness. No one else can see me shift back.

Fuck.

Rosalie books her flight and steps away from the computer. She's flying across the country to Los Angeles. And there's no way I'm going to be able to either be on that flight, or catch her tonight. Her flight leaves in three hours... and I'll still be a bear then.

"Be rational, Rosalie. You have your first big gallery opening in a few weeks. You can't miss that. It could be your big break in the art world."

"I can't get a big break if I'm dead," she says.

And I feel a little insulted. I know she can't tell her roommate the full truth, but dead? She knows I'm not going to kill her. That's what she's afraid of—that she'll live a good long time—as my mate.

What a horror show... having to be pampered and loved and spoiled and living in an expensive penthouse with a rich age-appropriate guy that most women would kill for, who would never harm you and only protect you. What a damsel. What a nightmare. How does she get through it? I'm still so annoyed that she's being this dramatic about this. That she's... *rejecting* me. She should just accept her fate like I have.

Fucking humans.

"They don't know what I look like, you can go in my place," Rosalie says. "Or maybe I'll be back by then. I'm not sure yet. I just know I can't stay here right now. I need to get away and think."

I wait outside the window until she's about to leave, then I climb down the fire escape and wait in the parking lot. Maybe I *could* drag her off. But could I do it without hurting her? She'll fight me. I know she will.

I watch her load her bags into the trunk of her friend's car. She's made arrangements for her own car which is still in the forest, probably parked somewhere near mine. She's convinced her friend not to drive her to the airport. The excuse was... "It's really late, you shouldn't be out driving by yourself this late." A neighbor will take Nikki to pick up her car at the airport parking garage tomorrow morning.

I know the real reason though. Rosalie worries I'm out here, she worries that her friend might be in danger from a crazed bear intent on staking a claim. I would like to say she's wrong about that, but I'm not sure. The longer the mating goes without completion the more unhinged I'm starting to feel.

She scans the parking lot and finally her eyes lock on mine. It's as though I'm her worst fears realized, and I hate that look on my mate's face.

I wish I could talk to her.

"Don't go, Rosalie. Please." But all that comes out are animal sounds.

"Cooper, is that you?"

"No, it's another random bear," I say. I don't know why I bother speaking when the words won't come out human.

"Forget about me. I'm not your mate. This is crazy."

She backs slowly toward her car door, and I can't stop her without hurting her, so I just watch helplessly as she gets into the driver's side and drives away. It takes everything in me to ignore the instinct to chase her. I need to get back to my own car and wait for the sun to come up.

7
COOPER

I wake tangled up in my family's bear skins. I fell asleep in my den, clutching Rowan's pelt. My twin brother was the last of my family, and now I'm the last of my line. Not the last of all bear shifters—it's not quite that dire yet. But it may as well be. Rowan is the reason I never wanted a human mate.

His rejected him and ended up dying before he could get her to change her mind, and then soon after, he followed her to the other side.

I think back to his last days, and my repeated pleas to him fill my mind.

"Rowan, you have to eat something."

"I just can't."

He'd wasted away. Finally, when he was near the end and had made the final shift into his bear form, I begged him one last time to eat... to live. For me. Why couldn't he live for me?

He laid a paw weakly against the side of my face and

pressed his thoughts into my mind. *Someday you'll understand, little brother.*

"I'm only three minutes younger than you!"

He made a chuffing sound that I could swear was a laugh, and then he was gone. I had to perform the rituals on my own. There was no one left. And now all that's left of my tribe is a bunch bear skins... and me.

My brother has been gone for five years but sometimes I still forget. Our team will win a game, and I'll pick up the phone to call him to go out and get drinks to celebrate... and then I remember.

And I'm going to end up just like him if I don't find Rosalie and get her to accept my claim. Humans are far too fucking fragile. I can't risk her dying before the claim is complete. I need to make her strong, like me.

8
ROSALIE

Los Angeles. *Two weeks later.*

It's been a couple of weeks since I saw Cooper in my apartment building's parking lot sounding for all the world like he was trying to reason with me—plead his case. But he has no case. I'm not going to become a bear. I'm just not. I have an art career to build, things to do.

He can't just *claim me* without me having any choice in the matter. It's too much like an arranged marriage for my taste. It somehow feels both like yesterday and a million years ago that all this happened, and a part of me is half arguing with myself about if any of it even happened at all. I know I must sound like the dumbest movie heroine in the world right now but really... shapeshifters? Were-whatevers? Vampires?

Those things just aren't real. They're fun to fantasize

about, but the reason they're fun to fantasize about is that there's absolutely no chance some supernatural hottie is going to claim you're his fated bride or mate and whisk you off to his castle. Because things like that just aren't real.

But he *was* real. If he wasn't, I wouldn't be hiding out in L.A. right now. Oh, sure, I was meaning to visit my sister anyway, but I wouldn't have taken a red eye... rushed away from my life... possibly run away from my first big opportunity as an artist if there wasn't a real thing to run from.

I sigh. He was hot though. And I mean, if it was just a casual fling? I'd be down for it. Aside from the psycho stalking—which maybe he can't even help under the circumstances—he seemed like a nice guy. In between alternately thinking he was crazy and fearing for my life and future, I felt a spark—that magical zap of electricity that shoots through your body as though you literally just got shot by Cupid's arrow.

I wonder if those are real, too. Let's hope not. I'm really not a fan of anybody but me being in charge of my fate. I'm sort of a control freak that way.

Katelin was surprised to see me that morning, bright and early at six a.m. But she didn't complain when I hobbled over her front door step all injured and pathetic. I kept looking around, afraid I'd somehow see Cooper, but no way could he be there.

Getting on a plane was the best way I knew to keep him from tracking my scent because I'm pretty sure a bear can do that. And I hoped that maybe in a few weeks he would have forgotten it. I mean, we've been living in the same city for who knows how long, and if he ever got a whiff of me, it didn't mean anything to him then.

So maybe he'll forget what I smell like. Maybe I can go back home, rent a new apartment, and go to my art show after all. I paint forests with sunlight shining through the trees and dappled shadows along the forest floor, waterfalls, bears, wolves. But I use a rainbow of colors in my paintings, not just standard browns and greens and grays and blues.

My sister is an actress. It's mostly national commercials and small roles in movies right now. A tiny speaking part here and there. She's got her SAG card. She's one of those actresses where you wouldn't recognize her name but if you saw her you'd be sure you'd seen her in something. And you probably have. Waitress number two. Girl running from dragon. Side character's baby sister. Fast food worker. And most recently: hotel maid who finds dead body. She had several lines in that one. I'm so proud.

She's got an industry party to go to tonight. Technically it's not fully a party, but just some people she's trying to network with all meeting up at a club, and she's convinced me to go out with her.

Admittedly I've been a little less down to party and go out than I normally am. I think in all the activity it's really just hitting me what a close call I had out in the woods, and I don't mean Cooper. But the combination of being attacked—even though that man thankfully wasn't able to complete his goal—and being stalked by a bear... well I'm not the same Rosalie that walked into the forest that day.

I'm a more cautious Rosalie. A less carefree Rosalie. A bit less innocent. I'd managed to stay off the radar of direct male violence for so long, and now... I don't know. But it's not something I want to talk to Katelin about. In the first place, I can't talk about Cooper, and in the second, if I talk about that man, it just makes it more real. And besides, he's dead. He's not a threat to me anymore.

If I don't tell anyone, it can disappear and fade into the background of my memories and no one looks on me with concern or pity to remind me of it. As far as my sister knows, I got lost and sprained my ankle in the woods, then inexplicably decided that was the time to get on a plane to California.

And my ankle is healed now, so I should go out. If I don't, Katelin will definitely start asking questions I don't want to answer.

"You're not dressed yet?" she says, coming into the guest room. She lives with her boyfriend, but he's out of town on a movie shoot. He's a slightly more successful actor she met when she was Waitress number two. You still wouldn't know his name probably, but you'd definitely know his face.

When they first started dating, she proudly informed me that those are his *real abs*. I'm not sure why she thought I would doubt his abs, but I guess with movie magic these days she just wanted to make sure I was aware.

Tonight she's wearing a black bodycon dress with gold strappy heels and a gold anklet. A long thin gold necklace disappears into her cleavage. She brushes away sun-kissed blonde hair to put in a pair of gold hoop earrings.

My hair would probably be blonde streaked if I was out in the sun as much as she is, but aside from my forest wanderings, I'm mostly an indoor person, so my hair has gone to a milk chocolate brown.

"Seriously, Rosalie, I can't be late. I know it's just club hopping, but I could get an actual character name this time," she says.

"Okay, I'm just not sure about this dress." I gesture at the red dress with thin spaghetti straps lying across the bed. It makes me feel like the flag you wave in front of a bull.

"What's not to be sure about? You'll look great!"

My sister and I are the same size—same size shoes, too. She helpfully picked out some black ankle boots to go with the dress. I didn't exactly pack club scene wear when I was tossing all my clothes into a suitcase like a mad woman.

By the time we get to the club, I feel more comfortable, a little more like my old self. Pre-Forest Adventure Rosalie. Party Clubbing Dress sold separately.

Katelin waves across the loud club, and some people wave back. She leans close to my ear and shouts, "Are you going to be okay if I go over there?"

"Yeah," I shout back. I mean not really, but I get how important these networking opportunities are for her to advance her career, and I did just drop in on her. And as far as she knows, nothing is wrong in my life. I just decided to spontaneously show up. She shouldn't have to rearrange everything for me when I can't even bring myself to tell her the real reason I'm here.

I successfully begged off going anywhere while my ankle healed, and I had a good excuse. But she didn't want to leave me alone tonight, and she already had these plans. So I'm going to suck it up and deal.

She weaves through the crowd to get to the group of men and women on the far end of the bar. I'm not sure how they can network in a place this loud, but sometimes it's just people liking and having familiarity with you that can create opportunities. It's how I got my first big show at a hot new gallery opening. Dumb luck and socializing.

Life's little opportunities rarely show up when you're huddled up inside your house.

I'm thankful the heels on the boots I'm wearing aren't high. My ankle feels fully healed, but I worry I could re-injure it if I step the wrong way. I start to move off the dance floor when someone comes up behind me. A male someone. My first instinct is to have an embarrassing freak out... but he smells... *wow* he really smells good. What *is* that?

It's strong yet subtle at the same time. Warm, musky. But also mossy. But somehow in a good way. I'm not sure I'm describing it right. I'm not sure mere words could convey it.

And the solid warmth of him pressed up against my back feels... comforting somehow. His hands skim my sides to land on my hips as he urges me to move with him. His erection grinds shamelessly against my backside as his arm wraps around my waist, urging me to press harder against his length.

It's a heady cocktail of that powerful scent, pure masculine strength, sensuous movements, and stark primal possession.

He hasn't spoken a word to me, and given recent traumatic events, I should be panicked, but all I feel is calm—and other things I'm going to ignore. Dark animal things.

I'm hit with a bolt of such overwhelming lust that suddenly I want this man more than anything I've ever wanted. I want him to hike up my skirt and fuck me right here in the middle of the dance floor. I want him to put me on my hands and knees and drive into me from behind in front of all these people—sweaty, writhing hot bodies that could never compete with the inferno building between us. I feel hot and cold all at once and the arousal between my legs thumps heavy with the beat of the music. The pornographic images flitting through my mind only grow stronger the longer we dance.

If you could call this dancing.

One of his hands has moved up to grip the front of my throat, holding me in place against him as he brings us impossibly closer. His other hand starts to slide up my thigh, under my dress, between my legs, his fingers barely brushing against the heat and wetness of my panties.

And then my fear starts to edge out my lust. No! I can't let this happen.

Forgive me if I don't want to just jump back out there and let a man touch me after... the woods. It's normal to feel a bit of disgust toward all men when one tries to hurt you like that. It almost feels shameful to let any man touch you ever again.

So why the fuck am I letting this stranger so close? Why am I rewarding any man for the bad behavior of his kind? Bad behavior I have personally suffered. I don't know him. He could be a fucking serial killer.

I come back to my senses and pull away. He grabs me and pulls me back to him, and instead of more fear, I feel a kind of rage I've never felt before. I stomp down HARD on his foot with my heel. He lets out a yelp, and releases me.

"Rosalie, wait!"

I shouldn't be able to hear him over the noise of the club, but I do. I turn around, and there's Cooper. I shouldn't be surprised. Didn't some small part of me subconsciously just know? It's why I didn't look back at him—just let him be a stranger, because the stakes are far too high with him as he really is.

He's wearing jeans and a black T-shirt that pulls tight over his muscles. His tattoos wind down his arms, ending just above his hands. Those warm brown eyes... that closely shaven beard... No. Absolutely not. His agenda might not look as bad on the surface as the guy from the woods, but it still involves his fucking boner... and controlling me. No. I'm *not* his mate. I'm not dealing with this alpha bro *You belong to me*, bullshit. I'm not going to just swoon into his arms because he's pretty and saved me, as though a man doing the decent thing somehow now obligates me to give all my freedom away to him.

Men really are just living on an entirely different planet.

And he doesn't get to just *decide* any of this.

I fight to get through the crowd on the dance floor, but his hand is around my wrist before I can get away.

"Let GO of me!"

A few people start to notice the conflict and back away, and I see a bouncer eyeing us. I'm pretty sure even as large as the bouncer is, that Cooper could take him.

He holds his hands up in surrender and takes a step back. "Just talk to me. I just need to talk to you." He gestures toward a free-standing circular booth in the restaurant portion of the club.

If he managed to follow and find me all the way out in California, he's going to keep following me. The time away hasn't dissuaded him. If anything, he seems more obsessed—which isn't great for me. Maybe I should just talk to him here in a public place and try to reason with him.

Finally, I sigh and nod and allow him to lead me to the booth. We sit. The acoustics of the club are such that all the noise and music are concentrated at the bar and dance floor. While we can still hear the music from our booth, it's a more distant faded sound so we don't have to shout to be heard.

Cooper scans the menu. "What are you getting?"

"This isn't a date."

"You still have to eat."

"I don't want you paying for my meal." I leave off the part about how I don't want him to feel like he's making progress with me, or like a tab is growing and the only way to pay the bill is spending a night in bed with him. But given what he's already told me and seems to fervently believe, I know it wouldn't be just one night.

He looks up and arches a brow. "Honey, you're my mate, of course I'm paying for your meal."

"I am *not* your mate!" I hiss.

"Take it up with fate."

He is so infuriating, but I choose not to make a bigger scene. Obviously I can't be this guy's mate, but I can at least be decent. He literally saved my life out in the woods, and he hasn't harmed me even though he had the same full opportunity that other man did.

A waitress shows up and I begrudgingly order a club sandwich and club soda.

"I'll have the same," Cooper says, handing the menu back.

He's friendly and polite to the waitress, but he doesn't ogle or watch her walk away. Am I keeping a points system in my head? This is not a date. This psycho bear is stalking me. He doesn't get the benefits of my points system.

"Do you not understand the word, *no*?" I ask him when we're alone.

He takes a deep breath. "Rosalie, it's not like that. Just give me a chance to explain."

"What exactly makes you different than that man in the woods?"

"I can't believe you'd ask me that."

"Well I am asking you that, so tell me, what makes your inability to hear no and his inability to hear no so different? Is it because you're hot? You think because I'm attracted to you that means I can't possibly have life plans that don't revolve around riding your dick?"

"I knew you were attracted," he says, grinning, and the dimple that appears near the corner of his mouth almost kills me.

I roll my eyes.

"This is why I wanted a shifter mate, not a human," he says. "Humans don't understand. And look, I get it, your males are fucking awful. I will be the first one to acknowledge it."

"Oh don't pretend like you care. I'm sure you all are the same with the female shifters, pushing your greater size and power around to get what you want."

Something in his face changes, and I can't pinpoint what emotion so quickly swept over him. But he doesn't leave me to guess. "Female shifters aren't physically weaker than male shifters, so no, we don't have the same power dynamics within our kind that humans do. I don't know why nature was such a bitch to human women, but it's not like that in a lot of the animal kingdom, and it's not like that with shifters. So whatever you think is going on here, understand I may look like a man, but I'm not one."

"But you're stronger than me, and you won't stop stalking me. So I'm not sure how I benefit from Shifter Social Politics."

He lets out a frustrated growl. A human sound, not an animal sound.

I sigh. "Fine, explain. What do you think I need to know that would make any difference at all to what I've already told you. You've made it clear you aren't going to leave me alone. So my options are just to "accept my fate" as you say. Why should I?"

The waitress returns with our drinks and sandwiches. That was shockingly quick, but sandwiches aren't exactly the most complicated cuisine. Cooper is silent while she sets down our plates and drinks, his eyes never leaving mine. I've stupidly left my hand on the table, and he reaches out to cover mine with his own.

I feel that same electric jolt that I don't want to acknowledge. This is some kind of magic, it's not real.

Really, Rosalie? You think it would require magic for you to want to sleep with this guy? THIS guy? Wow.

I could do without my brain's judge-y internal sarcasm right now. Whose side is she on?

His.

When the waitress has gone, I dig into my sandwich. Cooper just sits there staring at me. I've given him my undivided attention, and suddenly he has nothing to say. That's because there's nothing to explain. I'm about to point out this fact when finally he does start to talk.

"So, that day in the cave, you didn't believe me, and then once I shifted I couldn't talk to you anymore..." he trails off.

"Okay, so you tell me I'm your mate, but surely there have been people who reject their mate. What happens then?"

He gets a very uncomfortable look on his face before

finally looking away. And suddenly my imagination is going wild with the possibilities, none of them good.

"I just need you to give me a chance. I'll wait as long as it takes."

"For sex?"

He nods. "Sex, completing the claim, everything. I just need you in my house."

Oh sure, that's totally reasonable. I'll just move in with a stranger who stalked me across the country and has decided I'm going to spend the next several centuries in his bed.

I shake my head. "It's not that I don't find you attractive, Cooper. It's that I'm not interested in romance. With anyone. I have *goals* and you would be a distraction."

Yeah he would.

I really need my internal monologue to just stop talking right now. She isn't helping.

"What do you think I would prevent you from doing?" he asks, looking clearly confused.

"I don't know. I don't *know* you! But you would for sure slow me down."

I take another bite of my sandwich and stand. "I'm sorry, but no."

He grips my arm, and I just stare at him. "Let me ask you something."

"Okay," he says, not loosening his grip.

"Do you plan to keep me away from my family and friends?"

"Of course not." To his credit he looks horrified by the suggestion.

"Well, then you're going to have to let me go, because my sister isn't going to just not notice if I disappear. How do you think family gatherings will go if you kidnap me?"

He can't even deny it. He fully intended to just haul me out of here like a cave man. Finally he lets go of my arm and I get out of there. I text my sister and then arrange for a flight back home. I have an art show to prepare for, and if he can stalk me all the way out to California, there's no point in missing out on any more opportunities.

9
COOPER

One week later.

Everything inside me rebels against what I have to do, but I have to do it. I understand her perspective. It's not her fault fate spun the wheel and picked her as my mate. My sadness is not her problem to solve, and I know how it will look to her. I don't want her afraid of me, but she's so closed off. She will never let me get close enough to her to prove myself. I see that now.

I followed her out to California as soon as my bear form melted away. I stayed near her sister's house, watching, waiting, making sure she was safe and formulating my approach. When they went out to the club, I thought I could charm her or seduce her. But despite her attraction and the power of the mating link, she is the ice queen. She's never letting me in.

And I can't let her go.

Something will happen to her, and I won't be able to stop it. Even if she dies of old age or some other natural cause like an illness—it won't matter. As soon as she leaves this life, I won't be far behind her.

Rowan was right... I do understand now. It's all well and good to say romance doesn't matter. Having a mate isn't that important. After all, haven't I been fine as a playboy up until now?

But time has now been split in two. Before Rosalie and After Rosalie. And even though I don't truly know her, my soul knows her in a way so final and absolute that only a fool would try to deny it. I could try to go on with my life and let her go live hers, but I won't be able to live if anything ever happens to her. I need her strong. I need her human frailties gone. I just... need her to give me a chance to prove to her that I'm not a mistake.

Her gallery opening was a huge success. I had to wait and let her have that. She'd never forgive me if I took this from her. She doesn't know I'm here. I've been very careful to keep to the shadows, to stay out of her line of sight.

She's sold every painting. I bought one of them, but even if I hadn't, I'm sure it would have sold. It's a painting of a woman and a bear in the forest. It's us. Though the woman in the painting isn't a self-portrait of Rosalie, it *is* us. The bear sits behind her on the ground in a cold winter forest, hugging her from behind. One of the woman's hands squeezes one of the bear's paws in silent communication. He's her friend, her protector. Why would she paint this if she didn't want me? It seems like a clear signal.

Though I'm sure the signal isn't... *kidnap me and lock me up in your penthouse*, but still.

Rosalie is one of the last people out of the building, and she's parked at the far end of the parking lot. I don't let her see me. She's surprised, and I smell her fear when she breathes in the drugs on the cloth. I lay her carefully across the backseat of her car, and get behind the wheel.

10
ROSALIE

I wake abruptly, and it takes me a moment to puzzle out how I got here. The last thing I remember was walking out to my car on a high from selling all my paintings. I was a little sad to let the woman and bear painting go, and I refuse to think about what that means. I painted it last minute when I got back from California. It wasn't even finished curing when I took it to the gallery.

The image kept showing up in my dreams, and even though the subject matter disturbed me, I knew the only way to stop thinking about it was to paint it. Otherwise it would be the only thing I'd be able to see and I wouldn't get anything else done.

When the muse tells you to paint something, you paint it. If you try to ignore it and paint something else instead, you're only asking for a creative block, and I'd just recently broken out of one of those. I wasn't about to invite another.

I'm glad Cooper backed off. I am. We come from two

different worlds. And he is *not* the bear in that painting. It's just a bear. It doesn't mean anything.

I still don't remember how I got home and in bed though. I stretch and roll over. Wait... my bed is not this comfortable. I've needed a new mattress forever. There's a dip I tend to roll into, and yet... this mattress is firm all the way across. I stretch out like a starfish to prove my own suspicion.

And then I remember the parking lot and the foul smelling cloth going over my face. I bolt upright and look around. Yep, not my bed, not my house. I'm in an enormous lavish room with expensive yet understated furniture. It gives the vibe of *actual* rich, not pretending-to-be rich. A cream-colored leather sofa sits along one wall with a beige blanket draped over one side. The leather looks soft and buttery. Who has furniture this color? What if you spill something on it?

In this moment I've decided beige and white are wealth flexes because you don't need to hide stains, you'll just get another one! The entire room is done in these shameless neutral shades. The only spot of color is a large vase of pale pink roses on a table in the middle of the room—and at this point pale pink feels like just another airy neutral laughing all the way to the bank.

And... the painting.

The bear and the woman painting mocks me from just over the leather sofa.

Sun streams in through floor-to-ceiling windows, and I can see the city skyline. We are way high up. Well, he wasn't lying about being a rich werebear. Not that that changes anything.

Oh come on, Rosalie. A hot, rich, protective bear shifter just whisked you off to his castle and you want to go back to sharing a cramped apartment on the third floor in the bad part of the city? Sure.

Is there a way to murder my internal monologue without harming myself?

There's a knock on the door. I tense and just stare at it. I mean, I'm not going to say "Come in." That would be insane and seem like I was A-okay with this situation.

And how do I even know it's Cooper? Maybe someone else is fixated on and stalking me. I didn't see him last night. It could be anyone.

Yes, Rosalie, all the men want you. Every single one feels a strong and deep compulsion to take you as his bride. And they all have penthouses in the city. Aren't you just lucky?

I roll my eyes.

A moment later the door opens and Cooper walks in carrying a covered tray. His feet are bare. Jesus, even his feet are hot. He can't even have a single imperfection? He wears gray sweatpants slung low over his hips and no shirt. And even though I've seen him naked, somehow the little bit of mystery makes him that much hotter, drawing my attention sharply to that mouth-watering "V".

"I made you some breakfast," he says, like he didn't just drug and kidnap me.

"Are all shifters this... defined, or do you have to go to the gym?"

He smirks. "I work out." He says it nonchalantly as if it's no big deal to be chiseled like a Greek god.

He sits the tray on the bed, and that's when I notice the scent. What *is* that smell? I mean, I know it's Cooper. I smelled it at the club in LA. That warm, musky, woodsy, mossy... god it's driving me crazy. And it's stronger than it was in LA.

"Are you wearing cologne?" If he is, he took a bath in

it, but it's not too much. I mean it is definitely too much, but it isn't repellent. Quite the opposite, unfortunately.

"No, it's the mate thing. Only you can smell it."

I find that very hard to believe. How could anyone be in this room with him and not smell this? I catch myself before I crawl across the bed to him. What the actual *fuck*?

It's magic. I do not like this.

It's just so... compelling... Is it hot in here?

No, he's hot in here.

Shut up, brain. I do not need your input right now.

"It'll get stronger until the mating is complete," Cooper says. He puts the tray on the table next to the roses and walks to my bed.

Stalks like a jungle cat, you mean.

He sits on the edge and touches my arm. It's meant to be a light, comforting touch. I haven't even had a chance to yell at him for committing a felony. My brain is all scrambled by his nearness and scent.

And now that his warm hand is on me—even just my arm—I feel like I'm about to crawl out of my skin with need. The arousal building between my legs is embarrassing. He just touched my arm... for fuck's sake. He just *smells so good*.

My breathing comes out in sharp pants, and I'm sure if I looked into the mirror I would appear wild, my hair crazy from sleep, pupils dilated.

"Why isn't this affecting you?" I ask, warily. Maybe he gave me more than one drug? But no... this scent was affecting me all the way back in LA at the club.

He takes my hand and guides it to cover his erection. "It is, I'm just not fighting it."

I pull my hand away and jump out of the bed. Only now do I look down and realize I'm wearing pajamas. A pink cami top and little white boxer shorts with tiny red hearts on it.

I must look confused because Cooper says, "You have a whole closet full of clothes." He gestures to a white door that must be a walk-in closet.

He had to have been stalking me since LA to know all my sizes.

"I thought that was a bathroom," I say.

"The bathroom is a second door inside the closet."

Well, that's a unique layout option. I'm curious, and a part of me wants to check it out, but a bigger part of me wants to put as much distance between me and the bear shifter as possible, so moving into smaller and smaller spaces with no escape doesn't sound like a solid game plan if I want to reclaim my sanity and freedom.

A phone rings, and Cooper pulls a cell phone from his pocket. He holds a finger up in the air. "Yeah... I checked the online public records database, but the blueprints weren't there..."

I'm eyeing the door and wondering how distracted he is by his call.

"Yeah, I thought they might be in one of the boxes in the basement in the records room. Tomorrow's a bank holiday, but I'm working. Can you leave me a key at the office and the passcode? I'll swing by there after my meeting."

He's engrossed in his conversation and clearly doesn't think I'm a flight risk. I take one more look at him—because who can blame me—and race out of the room. I stop short when I get to the main part of the penthouse, momentarily caught off guard by what I see.

Holy shit, this place is huge. He has a grand piano in

the living room. Not even a baby grand, like a *grand* grand. And... a... a *waterfall*.

What?

I think my brain is short-circuiting. The floor-to-ceiling windows extend out here and to the massive kitchen. Everything in this place is neutrals. Clean lines. Grays and blacks and whites and beige with pale pink accents as far as the eye can see—mostly more fresh flowers—including but not limited to roses.

This guy must have a decorator. When we were out in the woods, Cooper didn't strike me as the kind of guy with an interior design degree. Or hell, maybe this isn't even his place. Maybe he broke in. Once you kidnap and imprison a woman, how much more of a stretch is it to steal a whole penthouse?

And... there are stairs that go up to an even higher floor. A two-story penthouse? Is that even a thing? I bet he has a pool and garden on the roof. Hmmm, *does* he have a pool and garden on the roof?

I decide I don't care and run for the door. But there is no door. I mean, there's a door, but there's no door knob. It's just a metal sliding thing like an elevator. I finally realize it IS an elevator. I must be still foggy from whatever he drugged me with last night because I swear I'm not normally this stupid. I can see now that the elevator opens directly into the penthouse, which, now I remember from movies is quite common. Not that movies are a window into actual reality.

Well, that's convenient, I guess.

I press the button but the doors don't open, and that little ding that elevators do doesn't happen. The button doesn't even light up. I jab it several more times in quick succession but nothing happens.

"The elevator only opens with my fingerprint," Cooper says.

I didn't even hear him enter the room. He stalks closer. I turn toward him, my back flattened against the cool metal of the elevator door, praying to melt through to the other side so I can ride the electric box down to the safety of the ground.

"Let me out of here." I try to sound firm and in control, but it comes out breathy. I feel panicked, like a deer in the middle of a field in the clear sights of a hunter.

"You don't want to leave." He slinks closer and that smell... god why does he have to smell so good, and look so good? I try not to stare at his tattoos or his abs or his... anything. But looking into his face isn't any better. He's just too overwhelmingly attractive.

"I, I do," I say weakly as he brushes a strand of hair behind my ear. And just this light touch has me wanting to straddle his leg and grind my pussy hard against it until I come.

No, No! I will not be doing that today.

Or *ever*!

He moves in like he's going to kiss me, and I come back to my senses. I shove him away, and he takes a step back. But it's clear he didn't have to take that step back. He's stronger than a normal man so my little human push certainly wasn't going to phase him.

"You lied to me! You said you'd wait as long as it took!"

"And this is how long it takes," he says.

I shake my head. "You knew this would happen if you got me in a closed space with you for long enough."

This wasn't happening back during the full moon in his den. I was attracted, sure, but I'm a heterosexual woman with a pulse. It didn't seem odd at the time—

despite the extreme circumstances. But the more time passes, the more intense his presence is. His smell, his...

He just stands back, studying me. He thankfully hasn't moved back into my space, but even as I think this, I want him to move back into my space.

"Do I smell like this to you?" I ask.

"I don't know what I smell like to you so I couldn't tell you. You smell like citrus and honey to me. And I love those two things. I'm using amazing restraint here, Rosalie."

I roll my eyes. "Yes, you're a model citizen drugging and kidnapping me."

He just shrugs. "It was what had to be done."

I choose to ignore this rationalization.

"I thought people have rejected their mates." To me that implied that they actually got away and got to go back to their old lives.

Cooper nods. "Distance will stop this intensity. That's why you're in here with me and not out there." He gestures toward the windows and the big outside world beyond them.

It's hard to imagine there's any world outside this space and this man even with the windows and view of the bustling city below to remind me.

He offers me his hand. "Now, come back to your room and eat something. That cover will only keep the food warm for so long."

I sigh, defeated, but I try one more time anyway. I feel like I need to. Yes, he's hot, he smells amazing, and this penthouse is incredible, blah blah blah. I'd be crazy to not want to live here, but I don't *know* this man. Life isn't a fairy tale or a rom com. A rich and attractive man can abuse you just as easily as a broke and ugly one.

And he's far too possessive for me to just trust that I'll be safe in his hands for centuries.

"Just let me go. You're rich and hot, you can have any woman you want." I'm not even trying to appeal to his ego. It's not flattery, just facts.

He smirks. "Except you, apparently."

11
COOPER

I'm questioning all my decisions right now. I know she wants me. That much is extremely obvious. The scent of her arousal perfumes the air almost as strongly as her growing citrus and honey mating scent. I wasn't kidding when I said I was using amazing restraint.

She's stubborn. And ordinarily, I'd like this character trait, but right now she's just causing herself far more mental anguish than she needs to. Once the mating is complete she'll understand... everything. Until that time, it's clear she's intent on driving both herself and me to the brink of madness.

I don't know how much longer I can smell that smell without just mounting her. The things I want to do to this woman...

All things she'll enjoy, of course.

"So, I have no choice?" she says, and I swear she's about to cry.

If she starts crying, I don't know if I can bring myself to keep her locked up like this.

You have to. Remember what happened to Rowan's mate.

The thing is... I lied just a tiny bit about the scent thing. It is true that other *people* can't smell the scents coming off fated mates, but otherworld creatures certainly can.

Rowan's mate ran from him and died at the hands of a vampire.

Some vampires are obsessed with what they call *gourmet dining*. There are a lot of different ways for a vampire to get the best, most potent flavor out of human blood, but the top delicacy is a human destined to be a shifter's mate, where the mating link has started but hasn't been completed.

The way she smells is the way she'd taste to them. And plenty of vampires would do more than kill for a human whose blood tastes like citrus and honey.

"Cooper? Did you just stroke out?"

I shake myself from my thoughts and mentally scroll back to the last thing she said... Oh yeah... choice.

"I don't have a choice either," I say, which really isn't the best *choice* of words. And I'm shown how clearly stupid these words are when her hurt gaze meets mine, and then her accusatory words follow.

"You don't even want me."

She is so wrong about that. "Oh I want you, Rosalie, but this would be so much easier if you were a shifter. Do you think I *want* to kidnap and terrorize my mate?"

"Maybe. I don't know your kinks." She tries to sound flippant but I know her trust in me is eroding every minute I keep her trapped like this.

"Well trust me, this isn't one of them," I say.

We remain in this stand off, staring each other down for several minutes until she says, "I'm going to go eat breakfast, and I want you to leave me alone. You have me where you want me, and obviously there's no escape."

Her gaze shifts to the emergency stairs.

"It's locked," I say. I had to install a deadbolt onto that stairwell door that locks both ways. It's a fire hazard, but either I lock her in her room or lock her inside the penthouse. So I chose the larger cage. Besides, if there was a fire, she could get to the roof and jump in the pool if I wasn't here.

"So, no escape," she confirms, defeated. "You need to honor your word and give me some space and time."

I sigh. I don't know how much time I can give her. The penthouse does buy us a lot of space from the threats to her, but if word gets out that she's not fully mated, I don't know if I can hold off those who would drain her of her blood.

And draining her isn't even the worst they could do. Some particularly self-disciplined older vampires will keep a destined human shifter mate alive for years, playing with them, feeding from them, restoring their health with their potent blood just so they can do it all over again. In many ways if a vampire were to get her, it would be far better for it to be a young one who would drain her and kill her right away. The older ones are much more creative and would break her in ways I don't want to think about.

I hold my hands up in surrender and just nod. She backs away, watching me the whole time until she's safely behind her door. I hear the lock click into place. I could certainly get in there but she'll get hungry again and have to come out eventually. It's better to give her some space. She just needs to be able to trust me.

I sigh and run a hand through my hair. Maybe I should

have just told her about the vampires. But I don't want her to be afraid or feel even more forced into this mating than she already does. And I thought it was pretty likely she wouldn't believe me anyway. I mean that story is just way too convenient... Give me exactly what I want for the rest of our lives or a vampire might get you. Yeah, that sounds like a real thing.

So here I am lying by omission to not look like a liar, so I can gain her trust. You can't make this shit up.

I've followed her, watched her, guarded her every night until sunrise since the full moon—a situation that is fast approaching once again. That's another issue. We really need to be mated before the full moon. It was fine when I first met her, but I don't trust the bear without the mating complete. He'll be... agitated, unpredictable. He wouldn't hurt her on purpose, but... I just can't predict what my animal side will do in this state.

Once the mate bond is complete, she'll be safe—both from me and from everything else. Vampires only drink from humans. No animals. No shifters. No otherworld creatures. Just humans. If my fated mate had been a shifter I wouldn't have to worry about any of this. But once the mating bond is complete, she won't be human anymore. She'll be off the menu.

Maybe I should just tell her. But then she really will feel like she has no choices. And she truly does not. If she refuses the claim, it's either be my prisoner for the rest of her life or die by vampire. And again, what the fuck am I going to do with myself on the full moon?

I'm just hoping the mate link does what the mate link does. The longer we're in such close physical proximity, the higher her desire and need will climb. Thankfully, male shifters stay at a relatively stable level of mating lust. It's the female that goes into heat to complete the claim.

And while Rosalie is a human and the heat isn't quite the same, it's still there. She won't be able to resist me for long. So there's no reason I need to bring up the vampires at all. Nature will take care of her resistance.

12

ROSALIE

Last night I dreamed I escaped the penthouse. It was all very dramatic and exciting, though the details live just outside the edge of my awareness —fuzzy and unreal. I somehow know it was so vivid while it was happening, but now in the day, I can't latch onto a single clear detail. I just know I got away.

It's been nearly a week in Coopers house. I tried to stay locked in my room in a battle of wills over if he'd just let me starve in here or bring me food. I was betting on the fact that if he's telling the truth about this mate bond thing, that he isn't going to be able to stand for me to suffer or go hungry.

That worked for the first couple of days—mainly because he had to go out during the day. Even though he's independently wealthy, he runs an architecture firm eight blocks from here, and while he can sometimes work from home, he had client meetings those days.

While he was gone, I was able to forage in the kitchen.

I took boxes of snack foods back to my room and squirreled them away under my bed, along with bottled water. I know how ridiculous this all sounds. I Know! Okay? I get it.

If it were you, you'd have swooned into his arms the very instant you saw him naked and let him fuck and bite you with wild abandon. Good for you. I'm not that way. I need... I need time. I need to get to know someone, trust them. I need to know how this is going to affect the rest of my life. Where am I going to paint?

Look, I get that he's hot. I get that he smells like something I want to climb. But no matter how wonderful he may be—and that's still largely theoretical—I can't spend my entire life just swooning over him and fucking. That's going to get boring... eventually... maybe in a decade. And then what?

I want to paint. I want to follow my dreams and build my career. I know artist fame isn't as glitzy as other types of fame, but I want it!

I don't want to be a *bear!* I don't want to give birth to baby bears. The idea of something with FUR growing inside me is just... I know some babies are born with hair on their heads but just... no. Okay? Just no.

Is he going to keep me barefoot and pregnant in the penthouse? Am I going to become Internet famous from my videos of making cheese crackers from scratch while wearing a 1950's housewife dress and pearls? Who can say?

How do I know he'll even let me leave if I complete the mating bond with him? Maybe he'll get even crazier. Maybe it's just a way to trap me forever.

For all I know, resisting him and waiting for my first

good opportunity of escape and then running until I can't run anymore is my only shot at a real life. He isn't the only hot successful guy that exists.

If he'd lock me inside his penthouse, is he even going to let me paint? And it's not like I can paint inside this glorious Architectural Digest centerfold spread with all the ridiculous white and beige. So where am I going to do it? Maybe up on the roof while the weather's still nice enough. But what about when winter comes? Am I expected to go a whole three months without painting?

He could probably spring for a studio rental, my logical brain supplies.

But probably not until I agree to the mating bond.

In the two days he was gone, I had a chance to really take a look at this place. The master bedroom is on the second floor, and it's enormous. There is a tiled floor and a giant tub inside the bedroom next to a huge window showcasing that glorious view. He has three walk-in closets and a master bathroom. I have no idea what the hell you put in three walk-in closets, but I found out. One was for casual clothes. One was for formal and business wear. And the last one was for his hobbies, of which he seems to have many.

The roof does in fact have a pool, a hot tub, a sort of cabana bar, and a small vegetable and herb garden. I'm sure he has some kind of help... a cleaning lady, a gardener, something. There is no way he keeps this all up by himself. And eventually that person is going to come here. And then I'll have my chance.

But... he's kept the place clean without anybody's help this week. I have never seen a man keep a space this clean. It's unnatural. He is fastidious... like a serial killer, which also gives me pause. I've checked his freezer but there's nothing suspicious—like human body parts.

Surely this neatness can't be a bear thing. I wonder if he hibernates in the winter. If so, do I just need to wait him out a few more months and then make my escape?

He also has a big grill up on the rooftop and solar powered string lights around the edges, supported by steel poles. Does he throw parties up here? At some point other people are going to be in our space. Right?

He confiscated my cell phone and he hasn't made the mistake of leaving any other phone in the penthouse, so I can't call the police. I push against the guilty feelings that rise when I think about getting him locked up. Besides, the full moon is coming soon, and I don't want to think about what would happen to him if he shifted inside a jail cell. But why should I have to be the one to sacrifice myself? Why should I feel guilty? Just because he saved me in the woods?

Nikki must be worried sick. When I didn't come home after the art show, she must have called someone. My family? Surely she filed a missing person's report. Is someone out there looking for me right now?

By the third day with him finally home all day and refusing to bring food to my room, I eventually had to come out.

The inexplicable primal need for him has climbed to the point where he doesn't even have to touch me to start my body humming. He just has to be in the general vicinity. I've masturbated probably twenty times a day since this thing escalated. Still, I resist him because this doesn't feel like my free will.

This must be how an animal in heat feels. He just has to be in proximity to me now. Even a shut and locked door doesn't lessen the need. I feel like I'm about to crawl out of my skin, and it takes all my will power not to beg him to take me. I have vivid full sensation dreams at night of his cock buried deep inside me as I buck against him and wail like some wild animal.

Each night, I wake from this dream with unbearable need between my legs, demanding my body surrender to him. All my senses are aligned in a mutiny against me, screaming for a satisfaction I won't give.

The first time I woke from this dream, I discovered the night table drawer beside my bed was filled with sex toys and a note: "Until you decide to let me take care of you. - Cooper."

I have no idea why he felt the need to sign that note. It's not as though I had questions about who left it. I'm sure with his super senses he heard the buzzing toys, and the sounds I made when I came. I'm sure he smelled me. And yet... he remained on the other side of that door, full of self-discipline.

Do I want him more than he wants me? That seems unfair. After all, I was the one who wanted him to just let me go.

I almost crumbled last night and begged him to fuck me. The arousal has gotten so bad when he's here, I can barely think. This penthouse isn't big enough if he's going to be... smelling like that. I don't know how much longer I can hold out.

And I can barely remember why I was trying to. Oh yeah... freedom and painting, and he might be secretly evil. I should write these top reasons of resistance down so I don't forget them again.

That brings us to today. He's out again. I think he had another client meeting. But he said he'd be back by sunset. And I can finally breathe. The sticky hot irritation of his hands not being on me has finally receded, and I feel somewhat normal in the calm peace of his absence. I'm only getting occasional mental flashes of his wet sudsy body in the shower now.

Oh yeah, that's another thing that's started happening these past few days. When he showers, I get these vivid technicolor mental pictures. And it comes with sounds and smells. It's like I'm in there with him. *Oh... Rosalie don't think that thought. Shut it down!*

I think he's sending me these images telepathically—in fact I'm sure of it. I remember the night I met him when he was in bear form and I heard "Mine" in my head. I thought I was imagining it, but I *heard* his thought. How could I not? He aimed it right at me. He wanted me to know. I would say that's not possible, but... given all the other fun new facts I've learned about reality, I've decided not to call anything impossible.

I heat up a bran muffin in the microwave and grab a glass of milk. Then I go up to the rooftop again. I'm starting to get cabin fever and need to be out in the fresh air. It's early fall and the air is crisp but not cold. I can still walk on the rooftop with bare feet and the concrete feels perfectly warm against my skin.

Not too hot, not too cold. It's weird to be so high up you don't have to worry about fallen leaves. Even in my third floor apartment, if I left the window open, sometimes a leaf would blow in during the fall months.

I know he's got a hot tub, but I wonder if his pool is heated, then I shake that thought away. I tell myself I'm not going to be here long enough to need a heated pool, even though escape seems futile.

I peer down over the ledge. We're thirty stories up, I

counted. And the elevator door won't open, no matter what I try. I've tried picking the stairwell lock with no luck. It's not as easy as they make it look in the movies.

I'm leaning over the side of the building when I hear some construction sounds below. Saws and hammers and drills on the floor just underneath the penthouse. The window is open. Actually it's not "open", because windows in high rise buildings like this don't open. It's a safety hazard. Nobody wants a small child to open the window and fall to their death.

The window is just... missing. They've started working on this floor. And they must have just started in the last few minutes because I would have been able to hear all this noise from the main floor of the penthouse, I'm sure of it.

I shout down. "Hello! Hey!"

A bolt of fear runs through me. These are strange men I'm yelling at, and I can't exactly tell them I've been kidnapped and am missing. For all I know they'll try to capitalize on my already "missing" state.

But then I reason that I'd just be asking them to call the cops. It's not like I could let them up here even if I wanted to. But what if the deadbolt on the stairwell door doesn't have a keyed lock on the other side? What if Cooper just installed that to keep me in but there's nothing to keep anyone else out? I have no idea about the layout of this building.

But the workers don't hear me for all the drilling and hammering and sawing. I decide not to yell again—at least not for now. Cooper probably won't be home until around six-thirty if his pattern on the other days he went in to the office holds. And I'm betting the construction workers will be off work for the day before then.

They'll take a lunch break, of course, but there's no guarantee they'll go off site to eat. They might just stay and have bagged lunches in their work space.

I go back inside and search through Cooper's closet. He may be rich and polished in one side of his life, but he's also a bear. He has wild in him. Nature in him. Plus he's very fit. That's a level of activity that probably isn't maintained with just two visits a week to the gym.

So I'm not at all surprised when I find not only a lot of camping gear but hiking and mountain climbing gear as well.

I can't possibly be about to do what I'm thinking about doing. It's completely crazy, and more than a little dangerous. I could die. Am I willing to *die* to get away from this guy? And why do I want to get away from him so badly again?

But then on the other side of the coin, why would I want to stay? He's keeping me in a gilded cage and even once I give him what he wants, there's no guarantee my circumstances will change. And this is not okay. This... civilized cave man routine. It's ridiculous to just throw my life away to live in a pretty cage with a hot guy.

Who *does* that? I blame all those princess movies we watched growing up.

I pull the equipment out of his closet and untangle the ropes and rappelling gear. Then I go downstairs and change into jeans and a T-shirt and some running shoes, because I will definitely be running in this adventure I have chosen. I just hope when I turn to page 132 that there's an ice cream cone and laughter and not a dragon waiting to eat me. Though the more likely horrifying scenario is just falling to my doom and splatting on the pavement outside. Lovely.

I find some cash on the bedside table in Cooper's room and stuff it into my pocket. I'll probably need to get a cab or something to get back home. I need to let Nikki know I'm okay, but I also probably shouldn't stay at our apartment. If he was a vampire he'd need an invitation to get in —assuming that's not a myth.

I'm not sure which formerly assumed fictional realities are true and which are not.

I wonder if there's someone who could do some kind of spell on my apartment to keep Cooper out or even mask my scent so he can't find me. But my mind immediately revolts against this idea. Shifters and vampires are enough supernatural elements. The idea that there could be witches and even more magic is something I don't even want to contemplate right now.

If I hadn't been forced to contend with the obvious magic of Cooper shifting into a bear right in front of me or the powers of the mating link, I'd still be denying the few things I've grudgingly allowed to co-exist in my reality.

I take the equipment I need up to the roof, and then I wait. I watch the clock all day, distracting myself in the meantime with food and TV. By midafternoon it occurs to me that I probably should know what the fuck I'm doing before I end up dangling off the top of a thirty story building.

He obviously hasn't left me with access to the internet, but I do find some mountain climbing and other nature magazines under his bed, so I skim the articles looking for information that will aide me in my escape.

Finally at five-thirty, all the drilling and hammering stops. I rush back to the rooftop and lean over the ledge to listen. I hear some muffled speech and then a door close, and then... silence. Still I wait. About ten minutes later I see men walk out of the building onto the street below.

I take a deep breath and look over the ledge again. It is so high up. But I have a way out. I wouldn't have been given this means of escape if I wasn't meant to take it. Maybe fate decided to let me out of this. Maybe if you can resist your fated shifter mate's glorious scent for six days in a row, you get a Get Out of Mating Free card.

If some mystical force of the universe can command you to be with someone for all eternity, can't that same force have mercy on you and give you a means of escape?

Maybe this is my opportunity to make a choice. To *have* a choice.

I get into the harness making sure everything is locked and snapped firmly into place, then I use some knots I learned years ago in girl scouts to tie the other end of the rope securely around one of the steel poles on the rooftop. I test the strength, pulling as hard as I can and forcing all my weight into it, but the pole doesn't budge. It is strong and firmly embedded in the concrete. And the knot is solid as well.

Okay... Rosalie, you can do this.

I think you should just stay and have hot mating sex with the growly bear shifter.

But I ignore that part of myself. That's the me who used to leave her drink unattended and went partying with strangers during finals week of my senior year of college. It's a miracle that me survived long enough to be in my current situation. That is not a smart or healthy me. Smart me, by contrast, has decided to rappel down the side of a building like I'm in an action movie. Totally sound choice!

It's probably close to six by the time I'm ready. I mean

nobody is ever totally ready for something like this, but as ready as I'll ever be. I've done the math on the distance between the rooftop and the windowless floor I want to end up at and made sure I have the right amount of rope —not too much, and not too little.

But I miscalculated the rope length, and now I'm eye level with the floor of the floor I'm supposed to be on. I panic. I do not have the greatest upper body strength in the world. I can't even do a full pull up, so even though I can reach the floor with my hands, I can't exactly just hoist myself over the ledge. If I were in a movie, I'm sure I'd be able to. It happens all the time... Young heroine has never spent a single day of her life in the gym training to do pull-ups, but when she falls over the ledge of the dragon's lair, she's somehow able to hoist herself up to safety just in the nick of time.

I will my heartbeat to slow to something approaching normal and then I lean back, grip the rope, and plant my feet on the side of the building like one of the magazine articles said to do. The honking traffic below reminds me unnecessarily that I'm basically in a sky hammock with very little separating me from my own grizzly death.

But I pull on the rope, lean back, and put one foot in front of the other, and somehow I make it the twelve inches I need to go to get back inside the building. I'm breathing heavily when I flop onto a bare floor covered in sawdust.

I remove the harness, get up, cross the room, open the door, and walk out into a plush green carpeted hallway like it's just a normal day. I avoid the elevator for fear of running into Cooper. I'm not sure how long that death defying stunt took, and he could be home any minute. Instead, I go to the end of the hallway, find the stairs, and jog the rest of the way down to the ground level.

Five minutes later, I'm standing on the street feeling like a certified badass. I hop into a taxi and reach my house just before dark. I'm about to put my key into the lock when a familiar scent assaults my nostrils and the blackness takes me.

13
ROSALIE

I'm awake and angry, but I refuse to open my eyes yet. I know Cooper is fast, but we must have just missed each other for him to be able to beat me to my apartment. This is so unfair. I made a legit heroic escape—like with background music and shit. And as soon as I get on my own home turf, before I can even get behind a locked door, he's recaptured me again. Seriously?

I may as well be a tiny turtle trying to escape a cardboard box. This is so fucked up.

But then I hear a male voice that is definitely not Cooper's, and the anger turns sharply to fear.

"Rodolfo, I thought I'd be able to sample her as soon as I rose for the night, but she just sleeps and sleeps and sleeps, doesn't she?" He sighs. "So annoying and inconvenient."

"We'll need to drain the drugs from her system before you drink, Sir."

"That won't be necessary. I'm not planning a full

feeding until tomorrow night. I just want to confuse the mating link so I don't have to worry about the bear."

Who... *the hell*... is that? I try to keep my breathing even and fight against the urge to open my eyes and satisfy my horrifying curiosity. It's now that I start to pay closer attention to my environment—the cold stone floor I seem to be sprawled upon.

"It's no use, poppet, I smelled the change in the scent of your blood. Fear. And your breathing changed... your heart rate changed. You humans contain very little mystery. You can't fake it with me, my dear, though you'll have plenty of opportunities to try."

Humans. My heart sinks at this word because I know that means he's *not* a human. And I'm not going to play dumb. I know what he is. Even before I open my eyes to look at him, I know. This room feels cold.

But not cold because of the temperature of the air. No, it's a deeper cold. It's a cold mixed with terror that seeps deep into your veins and takes up permanent residence there. I feel a loud internal scream inside my own mind, and I know.

Vampire.

His voice. The coldness both in him and in this room, it all screams to inform me of the predator I'm locked in with.

"Rosalie, come now, pet, let's not do this. You had your opportunity to choose the bear. And yet... here we are. What was it that gave you pause? Was it his good looks? His... what I'm led to believe is an absolutely intoxicating mating scent? You smell like citrus and honey by the way. Did he tell you? Absolutely irresistible. I cannot wait to really dig in and gorge myself on you."

I remain quiet. I still haven't opened my eyes. I can't

bring myself to face this new reality. So instead I just let him drone on as I shiver and try to stop my internal screaming.

"Or maybe it was his success? His talent? I hear he's quite the architect. His athleticism? His wealth? That luxurious penthouse? I can see why all of these things would be repellant to you."

A tear slips down my cheek, and suddenly I feel compelled to speak. "I just wanted to be free."

He chuckles. "That human curse. You can't take a good thing when it comes to you. No, you're all just full of ideals like... freedom. Hopes. Dreams. So cute."

Finally, I open my eyes, and I wish I hadn't. I'm in a large stone room that I swear is a throne room. It's all dark gothic design. It's exactly what you would expect a vampire's castle to look like—absolutely no mysteries to unravel here—though I assume it doesn't look like a gothic castle on the outside. I'm pretty sure people would notice that.

I'm lying on the cold stone floor, and he's sitting above me on what looks like a throne with a terrifying looking guard standing on either side of him.

He has cold ice blue eyes and a sneer on his handsome mouth. Oh, no question, he's hot. But he's evil—and not the good kind of evil. He's not the "villain... but not really". He's not the misunderstood beast who just needs to be healed by a good woman's love.

No, this guy is *empty*. There is nothing inside him to melt, nothing to fix. Nothing to reach. He feels older than the earth itself, and I know I have no hope of manipulating him.

"No, you really don't," he says. "I'm glad you're at least smart enough to recognize that, even if you weren't smart enough to do the one thing that could have saved you from me. Accept the bear's mating mark."

I feel somehow suddenly even more vulnerable than I did just a few minutes ago—if even my thoughts aren't private... what hope do I really have here?

"Did Cooper not tell you about me?" he prods, twisting the knife in deeper.

"He told me about vampires," I say, realizing the complete redundancy of even speaking to a man who can read your mind. And did Cooper really tell me about vampires, or did he just mention in passing that they existed?

"No, I mean me, specifically. Or maybe he just doesn't know. I killed his brother's mate. She was quite an entree. She tasted like red velvet cake. I admittedly have a weakness for sweet things. She was so good, I just gorged on her blood until she was no more. But... I like to think I've grown as a person since then. So don't worry, I plan to take my time with you—use restraint. Who knows... maybe you could be my pet for years... decades... centuries, even. My blood can keep you at just the right... *vibrancy*... for my taste—for as long as I wish."

No, Cooper failed to inform me of all of this. And now I'm back to being mad at him. Sure, now that I have a control in this experiment to compare with, Cooper clearly isn't evil. But, he might be a fucking dumbass. How could he not tell me about this?

And have you blame him even more for being forced into mating?

I wonder briefly if this is my own traitorous internal dialogue or if the vampire has pushed this thought into my head. But I know deep down, it's me finally seeing reality for the first time.

"You know, poppet, that death defying stunt you pulled to escape the horrors of being mated to a total sweetie pie like Cooper? That wasn't your idea, so I hope you aren't planning to claim it was."

He snaps his fingers like a hypnotist breaking his spell, and all at once the dream I had last night floods back into my mind, and I know it was only being held back from my awareness by the vampire. He slunk into my dreams last night. He gave me every piece of the escape. I followed his plan exactly as he'd laid it out, like some zombie acting out a play. It was all a trap.

I'm torn between relief that I don't have to blame myself for running away from Cooper this time, and disappointment that I only thought I was fully in control while I was planning and executing my escape. It felt so real. It felt like my idea. But even if it wasn't, I still did those things. There was no supernatural power that led to my success. I could have just as easily failed and fallen to my death.

The vampire doesn't seem interested in my mental hamster wheel; he just continues his villain speech.

"I've been tracking you since you returned from California. Unfortunately Cooper beat me to you... initially, at least. It was quite a puzzle to figure out how to get you out of a locked penthouse in the middle of the day when he was away, no less. I had to go to great lengths. The number of people I had to enthrall, well, you just wouldn't believe the work I've put in to acquire you. You should feel flattered. First there were the tenants just below you... I had to get them to move out, quickly and at the last minute. I had to get the building owner to go along with it, and then clear out the apartment as he just *happened* to decide he really needed to remodel everything and bring construction workers in. It was some of my finest work. And of course one of my human servants brought you to me once you were out in the wild again."

I can't stop the tears. I have nothing to say to this monster. And I know begging won't do any good. There is no humanity in him, so why bother?

"Oh, come now. You'll have wealth and luxury here, too. I mean, you'll eventually have luxury, once you've earned my favor. I don't just give out nice airy rooms for free, you know. I'm not quite so eager to please as your besotted mate." His dark gaze sweeps lewdly over me, and I know exactly how he plans for me to earn my nice room. "Eventually you'll grow to enjoy my touch, my bite, the feeding. It's all quite dark and erotic. I'll turn you into a completely new creature. And you'll forget all about silly pesky things like freedom and art. *Making* art, that is. I plan to expand your no-doubt subpar education on *real* fine art. I have some of the rarest paintings in the world in my collection."

I don't have any brave words. The banter that easily flowed between Cooper and me is absent in the face of this primeval threat.

He sighs. "I do hope you'll become an interesting conversationalist, poppet. It's really not enough to be young and pretty and have delicious blood. Are you understanding me? Are you mute? Speak!" He barks that last word out at me like I'm a dog.

"Yes, I understand," I bite out.

"Good. I would hate to have to just drain you, but if you aren't going to be the slightest bit entertaining, it doesn't matter how rare your flavor is. I'd prefer someone grateful for the opportunities I present. I'll show you the world. We'll travel everywhere. I'll put you in the finest clothes, keep you in the most luxurious lodgings. All you have to do is be a tiny bit agreeable and pleasant. Do you think you can manage that? I mean, it's only your life on the line here, after all."

"Yes," I choke out. Thankfully my inner voice has stopped taunting and judging me for my choices. For all I know, the vampire has been manipulating my mind from the very beginning.

"No," he says, "You don't get to put that on me. Also, I would start to guard my thoughts, if I were you. I can be quite sadistic when I'm displeased with a blood doll. Just something to keep in mind. Rodolfo?"

He gestures to one of his guards, and a moment later, I'm picked up off the floor and placed on the vampire's lap.

I shudder in his cold embrace as he strokes my hair as though I'm a pet he just picked up from the pound. And he probably does see me this way. He did call me *pet*, after all. It's such a vampire cliché, but I'm sure this is how he truly sees me. Just an amusement. Something to dress up in little Goth Barbie outfits. Someone to train to do tricks. There is no reality in which he would ever see me as his equal.

Cooper might be an otherworldly being, but he's not inhuman.

"That's because a shifter *is* part human," the vampire says. He can't even pretend to stay out of my mind, and I have no idea how to keep him out. What does *guard your thoughts* even mean? I can't just stop thinking.

He takes my chin in his hand and turns me sharply to face him. His fingers are long and elegant, and his grip is like a vice. He's very pale with dark hair and lips so red he looks like a goth who has painted his face with makeup, except that it isn't makeup. My heart rate picks up speed as it occurs to me that he may have already eaten tonight. How else would his lips have this much color? Did he kill them? Did he...? I refuse to let my conscious mind complete this thought, but he picks up on it anyway.

"I did, as a matter of fact, feed already. I fucked her on black silk sheets and then drained her of all her blood. She was such a pretty thing, and she screamed so sweetly for me. That moment where screams of pleasure turn into screams of pain... and then it all dies out on a whimper and a gasp... I never get tired of it. And then those sightless eyes that still carry the trace of shock that it all ended this way. I mean, come on, how could the little twit not know I was a vampire? But she was a cheap fast food hamburger, you—my dear—are a delicacy. It won't be so quick for you."

I can't stop the tears moving down my cheeks. I would give anything to go back in time, to not run from Cooper. I thought I could just rejoin the normal world. I didn't know I was now a permanent part of all this. I didn't know the dark places my life could go.

"You'd be wise to forget about him. It's unfortunate, but sometimes we make choices in life that we can never really undo. We just have to live with them. You'll never see the shifter again. After I bite you, he won't want you anymore. Even if he could find you, he would discard you as soon as he knew a filthy vampire had defiled you. And I plan to defile you in every way a person can be defiled. So you might want to do whatever a human needs to do to prepare themselves for such a stark ongoing reality."

Can't he just fucking shut up? I know villains like to talk, but just... *shut up!*

I'm sure he heard that thought. I'm sure his guards

also heard that thought, given the force with which I delivered it. In the next moment, he strikes. I cry out at the searing pain of fangs in my throat. He grips my shoulders as he drinks. A moment later he flings me away from him and spits the blood out on the concrete as though he's disgusted.

So much for being a delicacy.

I press a hand to my bleeding throat.

"Ugh. Those drugs are rank," he says.

"I offered to drain the drugs off, Sir."

The vampire waves him away. "Just close her wound."

"Yes, Sir."

I shrink back as the hulking guard comes closer. His eyes glow briefly red. I had thought he was human. Is he a vampire, too? He pulls me into his arms, and I cringe as he licks the side of my throat.

Then he gets up and returns to stand behind his boss. When I touch my throat again, my hand comes away clean. No bleeding.

"Well? Put the puppy in her crate, she's useless to me until the drugs have cleared. I'll feed and play with her properly tomorrow night."

Rodolfo comes back and picks me up off the floor. Before we're out of the room, my captor speaks again.

"Poppet, do you know what tomorrow night is?"

When I don't answer, he fills in the blank.

"The full moon. Even if he could find you, he's not going to be able to control the beast when he smells me on you. He might just kill you himself. Wouldn't that be ironic? You needing *my* protection from *him*. I've never gotten to play the hero before. It might be amusing."

With that pronouncement, Rodolfo is dismissed with me in his arms. My *crate* turns out to be a cell with a mattress on the floor and a toilet. There's a mini fridge on one end of the room with what I hope is food and water inside. A large red digital countdown timer hangs on the wall. Twenty-two hours, thirteen minutes, and nine seconds. Eight... seven... six...

Rodolfo speaks then. "That's the amount of time until the sun sets tomorrow. Marcus will return for you then."

The vampire's name is Marcus, and he's helpfully given me an exact waiting time until my life goes completely to hell, and the real nightmare begins.

14
COOPER

T*hree hours ago.*

It's just after sunset when I reach my building. My heart hammers in my chest as I get onto the elevator.

You're being ridiculous, Cooper.

But I don't believe my own self talk. It's not ridiculous to not want Rosalie to be alone even a minute past sunset —not with what's out there. A vampire doesn't need an invitation to get into a human dwelling. And even if they did, my penthouse *isn't* a human dwelling.

I watch the elevator numbers go up so much more slowly than normal. *Come on. Come on.*

What do I think could have happened? I don't even know if there are any vampires in this city. I don't know if anyone caught her scent and put the pieces together. She's so high off the ground that surely she's out of any otherworld being's scent range. It's the only good part about keeping her locked up like this until the mating. So why am I so upset my meeting ran late? Why am I so on edge?

It's the moon, dumbass. It's just the moon making you crazy. Don't forget that's how we got the word lunatic. It even affects the humans.

I sigh, that's true. Of course that's true. It's a reasonable explanation for my unreasonable panic. It must just be the coming moon. I need to be focused on trying to get Rosalie to let me complete the claim before the full moon. Maybe I should have picked up something more romantic for dinner—like spaghetti and meatballs and wine. I should have been more focused on woo'ing her instead of respecting her space. But I know my scent is affecting her. She'll cave soon. The question is... will she cave soon enough?

The elevator opens on the penthouse level.

"Rosalie, I brought home some burgers." I am such a failure as a Woo'er. My shoes echo over the marble floor. I put the bag of food on the counter. "Rosalie?"

She's not in her room or on the main floor. I race up the stairs to find my closet has been ransacked. The money on the nightstand is missing.

"Rosalie!" I climb the final set of steps up to the roof. I'm panicked, but I've also convinced myself she's just having a drink from the cabana bar or maybe she's in the hot tub.

I feel my eyes glowing and a partial shift coming over me when I find the roof as empty as the rest of the penthouse. I glance down to see my claws fighting to push through. I take a long slow breath.

Relax. Relax. Relax.

It isn't as though I can do full shifts without the direct power of the moon.

After several tense minutes I feel my eyes go back to normal and my hands are once again just hands.

How could she have gotten out? Or did someone else get in? What if she's just in the bathroom and I'm being crazy? I go back downstairs to check her bathroom, but the penthouse truly is empty. There's no sign of forced entry, and no one could have gotten up to the penthouse without my literal thumbprint. I go back to my closet and notice the rappelling gear is missing.

Back to the rooftop.

My heart drops into my stomach when I see the glint of rappelling gear and the rope tied around the pole. There isn't enough rope to get to the ground. And if she'd fallen, the entire perimeter of the building would be roped off with police tape. Unless it just happened.

I take a deep breath and look over the edge. And that's when I see the missing window. I pull up the rope, get into the harness, and climb two floors down.

I can smell her here. Okay, so... she ran away. That's better than the alternative. I just have to get to her. I'm going to have to tell her about the vampire threat and just hope she doesn't think it's some made up bullshit to trick her into accepting the mating.

I eat my burger on the way. I barely ate today, and I can't be half-starved when I reach her. I'm irrational when I'm hungry.

But when I reach Rosalie's apartment building and get out of my Jeep I don't smell her—not in the parking lot, and not at her door or window. More importantly, I don't *feel* her. And that's when I really lose it.

She could have gone somewhere else, but why don't I *feel* her?

I should feel her. Even when I'm away from her, there is this ephemeral thread of connection that I can sense like some piece of her is always with me. Did it just now break? When did it break?

She's dead. I lost her.

I begin pacing the parking lot like a mad man. I want to do something but there's nothing I can do. Do what? Resurrect her? I don't even think that magic works. And even if it did... she'd come back wrong.

I spend about fifteen minutes having what I'm sure must be something halfway between a panic attack and a nervous breakdown. And yet... the grief doesn't come.

She's my *mate*. Where is the crushing grief? All I feel is anxiety. And that's when it occurs to me. She's not dead, she's been *bitten*. That's why I can't feel the link! I race to her apartment and bang on the door.

Otherworld beings don't share our reality with humans. Humans cannot be trusted. The only humans we ever let in are mates. But I'm the last of my line, who's going to stop me? I need something of Rosalie's and her friend is just going to have to learn about magic today.

"What the hell?" Nikki says when she opens the door. I smell food coming from the kitchen. I've clearly interrupted her dinner.

"I need Rosalie," I blurt out. *Great, job, Cooper. You sound like a psycho three year old.*

And that's when her face changes, and I notice her red-rimmed eyes. Fuck. Yeah, her friend has been missing for almost a week and I didn't even let Rosalie call anyone. In my defense I didn't think it was going to take this long to complete the claim, and I didn't trust her not to yell into the phone that she'd been kidnapped. But seeing what this has done to her friend, combined with how I'm feeling right now. Yeah, I'm an unforgivable dick.

She looks like she's about to start crying again.

"I know where she is," I say. I mean that's not exactly true. I don't know where she is or I wouldn't be here right now trying to negotiate my way into a human's apartment. The clock is ticking, and I don't know how much time Rosalie has, but if she's still alive after being bitten, whoever has her doesn't intend to kill her immediately. This realization stresses me out even more. I don't want to think about all the things a vampire could do to her—especially a vampire with the self-control to bite but not kill.

Nikki's initial annoyance-turned-to-grief has now shifted to suspicion.

"You took her! You're the man from the woods, aren't you? The man she was fleeing from."

What can I say? All that is true, technically. "I can explain," I say.

"I'm calling the police."

I push my way into the apartment before she can shut the door on me, which I know obviously isn't a great way to gain her trust, but we can't have this conversation outside in full view of possible passing neighbors.

She races to the kitchen and grabs a giant knife.

I hold up my hands in surrender. "Please, just listen to me. Just hear me out. What I'm about to tell you is going to be hard to believe."

"You sick, psycho. Why did you take her?"

"She's my mate."

"What does that even mean? You're fixated on her or something?"

I can't just shift and show her. Though honestly that would probably scare her more.

"No. I mean... no, I'm not fixated." The more I try to explain this, the worse it will be.

My gaze shifts to the wooden block that holds all her kitchen knives. Her gaze shifts there as well. We both race for it, but I beat her there and pull out a knife of my own. I jump out of her reach as she slices at me.

"Nikki, I need you to calm down."

"You're a psycho stalker with a knife. I will *not* calm down!"

"I need you to just listen. I'm going to tell you something that's going to sound crazy, but I can prove it, so just watch."

She still has her knife raised, but I at least have her attention now. She isn't about to look away from the knife in my hand. I decide a visual demonstration is easier than explanation first.

I raise the knife and slice it down my forearm.

She gasps, horrified. This was clearly not what she was expecting me to do with the knife. I'm also kicking myself for not giving Rosalie this demonstration originally back in my den. It just didn't occur to me at the time—not that it would have made much difference.

"Nikki, watch."

I point to my arm. Her gaze follows to watch as the wound seals itself.

She shakes her head. "It's a trick."

"It's not a trick. How would that be a trick? This isn't stage magic. You literally just saw me heal right in front of you."

The human mind is ridiculously stubborn at accepting any reality that doesn't match its current programming—

something which often benefits the otherworld, but isn't nearly as convenient right now. In general we don't worry that much about the humans seeing some bit of unexplainable magic because they never trust their lying eyes anyway.

"How did you... How... What..." Finally her gaze raises to mine. "What *are* you?"

Oh good. We've finally reached the explanation portion. And she at least is quickly coming around to the idea that I might not be fully human. It's a start.

"I'm a bear shifter."

She wrinkles her nose. "A werebear... like a werewolf?"

I roll my eyes. "We don't say *were*, but sure. About a month ago on the full moon, I was out in the woods... doing bear things, when I heard a woman scream. It was Rosalie. A man was attacking her."

"The man she was running from?" Nikki says, trying to understand and put the pieces together.

I have to at least give her credit for making an attempt to understand all this instead of screaming and throwing all her kitchen knives at me—not that that would do anything.

"No, she *was* running from me." I probably shouldn't have said that part.

Nikki raises her knife again, and I raise my hands—minus my own knife—in a placating gesture. I really need to work on my compulsive honesty.

"Wait. I killed the man who was trying to hurt her. She fainted, I realized she was my fated mate, and I brought her back to my den. The next day I told her all this, and the very short version is... she ran away."

"So you kidnapped her," she says.

"Technically, yes, but only for her own safety. So this wouldn't happen."

"So what wouldn't happen?"

I'm losing patience for this back and forth. Rosalie is out there, and I don't have time for a slide show right now. So I just say it. "I think she was taken by a vampire. He bit her and now I can't find her through our link, so I need a personal item of hers to take to my witch friend to try to find her." My panic dampens slightly as I realize just how insane all of this sounds. Even after witnessing my magic healing, I'm not sure she'll be on board, and I don't have time for this.

But apparently my brief bloody demonstration was enough for her because the next words out of her mouth are... "I'm coming with you."

15
COOPER

The ride is tense. Nikki sits in the passenger seat with a necklace from Rosalie's jewelry box and a sweater. She couldn't decide which item was more personal, so she brought both. She clutches the sweater in her hands, her knuckles going white as I weave in and out of traffic.

She's clearly rethinking all this. I can't read minds, but she's thinking loud enough that I can almost hear her thoughts. Or maybe it's the combination of her posture, her scent of fear, and the way she keeps looking over at me. I assume she's just now realized that I could be an otherworldly creature and *also* a liar, and that maybe all her initial fears were true.

"Where are we going again?" she says, breaking the silence. And I'm sure she thinks I'm about to cackle and say: My evil lair.

"To see an ex of mine."

"What?" She turns in her seat toward me, her fear shifting to exasperation.

"She's a witch. I told you that. We need her to find Rosalie."

Nikki is still processing the supernatural world. I can't blame her. It's a big reality shift.

After another twenty minutes of fighting traffic, I turn off the engine in a parking lot on the edge of the city. We're sitting in front of a green building with a blue neon sign that reads, "Coven Mart."

Selene has a strange sense of humor.

Nikki just blinks at the building. "Was this always here?"

"Yeah, but she's got a light cloak on it. Most people don't really notice it. Those who do tend to be humans who do some version of what they call magic, but don't actually have otherworld powers."

"But this witch does?"

I nod. "This witch does."

Selene gets a kick out of having a witch store selling stuff to normie humans that most of them don't really know how to use. Witchcraft has gone mainstream enough that at least that part of the otherworld doesn't have to be completely hidden. It hides in plain sight. She's loving this ability to mix and mingle. Just a few centuries ago, her family barely escaped a witch burning purge—so she's enjoying this new sense of freedom.

I glance at the clock on the dashboard. It's already eight-thirty. The shop closed half an hour ago. We get out of the Jeep.

"Maybe I should just wait out here," Nikki says.

"No. You're coming inside where it's safe. Vampires, remember?"

She looks around, uncertain, but follows me up to the

door. I bang on it. We wait. I bang some more. Finally, the door opens.

Selene looks the same as always, long flowing black hair, a black corset, black mini-skirt, fishnets, combat boots, and dark red lipstick painting lips that always seem to smirk in a knowing way.

"Well, if it isn't Cooper Blackmore. I knew you'd be back. I should make you work for it, but I know what you can do in the bedroom, so I'll forgive you this once." She licks her lips as her gaze slides down to a package she was once well acquainted with.

She finally notices Nikki. "Who the fuck is this? You know I don't do threesomes unless it's another guy." She raises a hand, and I know what that fucking wrist flick can do, so I grab her by the arm before she can do damage.

"She's not important. I need your help."

Selene jerks out of my grasp and rolls her eyes. "And why should I help you?"

"We broke up three years ago! You can't still be mad about it, and you of all people should know it wasn't ever going to work."

"And I told you, I could do a spell that..." I cut her off before she can re-explain her plan to block any future mate connection from forming at all, so she and I could be together—so we could cheat fate. But despite all that comes with it, I wanted a true mate.

"Selene, I found my mate."

Her eyes narrow into slits, and I'm not entirely sure I'm going to survive the night.

"Congratulations, I'll be sure to send a mating gift." She starts to slam the door in my face, but then she senses it.

She turns on me like a hungry jackal, a sharp satisfied

gleam in her eyes. "Uh oh... your mating isn't completed. What happened... did she run from you, Cooper? Did you scare the poor thing with your..." she gives me a long slow once over. "... stamina? Wait... is she *human*?"

This is why we're here. Selene may be difficult, but she's powerful, and when she can get out of her ego for five minutes, she senses... everything.

"She's been taken, and I need your help."

Selene laughs. "You need *my* help. I'm sorry, have you met me? I'm not exactly the charitable type. And I'm jealous and vengeful to boot, or did you forget that in our time apart?"

"Believe me, if I knew *any* other witch, I would go to them. But I don't. And the fact that there are enough wannabe witches in this city to keep you in business, means I'd have to vet through a lot of humans to find an actual otherworld witch. And I don't have time for that."

She looks at me, *really* looks at me, and I could swear there is something like pity in her eyes. "You should have let me do that spell back when it would have worked."

"Please, Selene, help me. You know what we had was nothing more than a good time."

"To you, maybe."

"Either way, it's too late for that, and you know it. You know what will happen if I lose her, so if you ever cared for me..."

She sighs. "Fine. Come in."

I hold the door open for Nikki and then step inside behind her. We follow Selene to the back room and up a narrow set of stairs to her apartment over the shop. The most remarkable thing about Selene's apartment is how utterly unremarkable it is. Nothing about it screams Witch In Residence. Even the most skittish human would never suspect Selene lives in an extended love affair with the dark arts.

"Did you bring something personal of hers?" Selene asks.

Nikki meekly holds out the sweater and necklace.

"I don't need all her stuff, hon." She snatches the gold heart-shaped locket. "This will do."

She plops down on her ass in the middle of the living room floor without any preamble, candles, or spooky lighting. If I didn't know her I wouldn't take this seriously, but she doesn't need any of the props and spectacle to get shit done.

She holds the necklace in her hands and chants softly, rocking back and forth. Then her eyes go solid white as her head shoots back. I may not be magic in the same way she is magic, but I feel the energy in the room shift, and it seems Nikki feels it as well.

After what seems like a small eternity, Selene comes out of her trance and hands the necklace back to Nikki.

Nikki hesitates.

"It won't bite you, sweetheart. There's no scary magic on it or anything. I didn't hex it if that's what you're worried about."

She tentatively takes the necklace back and puts it in her pocket.

"Well?" I say. "What did you see?"

"Your girl's alive, and safe enough—for the moment. She's being kept in a cell. There's a timer on the wall, which I assume is when he plans to come back for her. Just some old-fashioned psychological torture. I heard some talk from one of the guards. Marcus only bit her tonight to mute your connection. Guess he didn't know you knew a strong witch. Either way, he's not going to touch her again until tomorrow night when he rises. He's waiting for the drugs to wear off."

"What drugs?"

"Well, I'm not a pharmacist, Cooper, but I assume whatever drugs were used to transport her to him."

I start to pace. Marcus. I don't have to ask if it's the same Marcus. I push down the growl bubbling in my chest.

"I thought that motherfucker was in Europe?"

Selene sighs. "He's a vampire. You know how nomadic they are. Maybe he got bored."

"Where's Rosalie?"

She shrugs. "Your guess is as good as mine."

"Selene…"

"I can give you a general area, maybe within a few miles, but I can't do better than that. He's got wards, Cooper. Good ones. He doesn't want to be found."

"Then how could you see all the rest if you can't see where he is?"

"Because finding a conscious being is energetically easier than finding a physical location."

"Why?"

"I don't know why, Cooper, they didn't cover it in witch school. Why is the sky blue?"

"Because the sunlight is scattered by gases and particles in the earth's atmosphere," I say.

She rolls her eyes.

"Can't you just… break the wards?" I say.

"Let me put it to you this way, Mars needs to be in retrograde, and I need virgin tears. That's six weeks away, and it's also assuming I could find a virgin. Do you want to let your mate wait for me to be able to break his wards? What all do you think Marcus could come up with to do to her in that time? The imagination practically buckles under the possibilities."

"You don't need all that to do magic."

"Correction, I don't need all that do to magic unless there's another powerful witch involved... then I need to break out the spooky rah rah. I'm sorry, Cooper, I don't write the rules of magic, I just live by them."

I'm not entirely sure I trust her. And I wonder if she's just doing this shit to spite me. Maybe she'd prefer both Rosalie and I die, than to have to live with the idea of me with someone who isn't her.

She sighs. "I really can't pinpoint the house, Cooper. I'm sorry. But I can find the general location. Just give me a minute."

We wait as she goes into another room. A drawer opens and shuts. Another drawer opens. There's the sound of papers rustling.

"Ow, fuck me!" she hisses after she bangs into something.

Finally, she returns with a folded paper map of the city. She unfolds it and places it on the floor then holds her hand out to Nikki.

"What?"

"The necklace, dear. I need it."

Nikki digs the locket out of her pocket and passes it to Selene.

"I have to brew tea."

"Selene..." I growl.

"Cooper. Enough! I told you, he has wards. They're strong enough that I know I can't pinpoint his exact location without much stronger magic which requires celestial alignments we don't have right now. I'm so sorry this inconveniences you, but to even get in the general neighborhood, I'm going to have to do a little more, ritually speaking. Now be useful and go downstairs to the shop and get me a bloodstone, some ginger root, and mugwort."

Selene dismisses me and goes to her own kitchen cabinets to pull several amber glass jars from the shelves.

Nikki comes with me down to the shop as I collect the ingredients. I don't blame her for not wanting to stay behind.

Half an hour later, Selene finally has her tea brewed, some weird smelly herbs to sprinkle, and candles lit. The lights are dimmed and the map is spread out on the floor in the center of the room. She drinks the tea.

Some more chanting happens, and then she hovers the necklace over the map. It starts to move, and she seems to sense where to go so that the locket can find the right location. Finally, after testing several spots, the locket starts to move in a very clear circle.

Finally, Selene puts the locket down, leans back, and reaches into a drawer. She pulls out a red Sharpie marker and draws a circle on the map.

"There. She's somewhere inside that radius."

"Are you sure?" I ask.

She just looks at me like I'm quite possibly an idiot.

"Can I take the map?"

"Of course you can take the map. Why else would I draw the circle on it? As a souvenir of the time my ex asked me to help him rescue his one true love?"

She gets up off the floor, folds the map, and snuffs out the candles.

"How am I going to find her? This is still a lot of ground to cover." The circled location covers about five miles on the outskirts of the city—in the suburbs.

"Well, use that big architect brain of yours. There aren't a lot of basements around here. But a vampire's safe house will always have a basement."

I nod. "Thank you," I say with sincerity. "I know you didn't have to do this."

"No problem. That'll be $25,000. I take all major credit cards." She holds out her hand.

"You've got to be kidding me."

"No, Cooper. I'm not kidding you, and I know you can afford it. I need new plumbing in this dump. You broke my heart, and then you came to me to do magic to find the woman you plan to spend the rest of your existence with. That's expensive magic. And it'll get even more expensive if I have to put your account into collections."

"What does she mean by that?" Nikki says, her tone wary. Rosalie's friend has been quiet and attempting to blend into the background practically the entire time we've been here, a smart strategy to be sure.

"She means she'll hex me if I don't pay her."

"You always were smart," Selene says.

I pull out my wallet and hand her my black card.

She smiles broadly at me as she takes it. "Give me one moment to process your order and get you your receipt."

Nikki and I follow Selene downstairs back into the shop. She puts the map into a logo-printed brown shopping bag with black tissue paper that has silver foil stars on it, then runs my card. A moment later, the receipt prints.

Selene smiles sweetly as she passes me the bag with my card and receipt inside. "Thank you for shopping at Coven Mart. Have a magical night."

16

COOPER

"I'll drop you off at your house," I say to Nikki once we're back on the road.

"What? No! I'm not going home. I just watched a real witch do real magic to find my friend who's been kidnapped by a vampire, and you think I'm just going to toddle on home?"

I shrug. "Suit yourself, but you aren't coming to the house when I find her. It's far too dangerous, and I can't be distracted worrying about you."

She looks like she might argue, but if she didn't want to go into Selene's building, she really doesn't want to walk into a vampire's lair. And we both know it. "Okay, but I can help you find her."

I nod. It would definitely help to have more than one person on this job.

The drive is silent for about five minutes, and then Nikki turns in her seat toward me.

"You know the seatbelt doesn't do it's job when you twist around like that," I say.

She ignores me. "So have you and her…" She makes a juvenile hand gesture.

"If we had, she wouldn't be with a vampire right now because I would have marked her."

"What does that mean?"

I sigh. I don't want to do twenty questions right now, but it distracts me at least from what Marcus could be doing to her. Rationally, I know Selene's right. He's waiting for the drugs to clear, and whatever plans he has for her, he'll want to combine it with blood drinking. It's the vampire way.

If they party there's blood drinking. If they're fucking, there's blood drinking. If they're torturing… there's blood drinking. It's a clear and defined pattern.

I glance at the clock on the dash. It's already almost ten-thirty. I hate the idea of Marcus awake in the same building that Rosalie is in—even if he won't touch her again until the sun sets tomorrow. It still doesn't give us a lot of time. And I shift tomorrow night, which makes everything that much more dangerous.

"Hey! Cooper!" Nikki shouts, snapping her fingers next to my face.

"What?"

"What does that mean? Marking her?"

I'm sure Rosalie's friend is going to love this. "I have to bite her and mix our blood while we're having sex."

She's quiet for a long time. I'm not sure if her mouth is gaping open because I'm watching the road and trying to keep us between the lines. Finally she says, "What do you mean mix your blood?"

"I'll bite her, then bite my tongue, and then seal her wound."

"What do you mean… seal her wound?"

I swear it's like being in the car with a toddler. So I just ignore her and focus on driving.

Finally after several more minutes of blissful silence, she says, "What's going to happen to Rosalie?"

"Nothing. I'm going to find her." I have to keep telling myself this. I have to believe I'll find her before the sun sets tomorrow.

"No, I mean, what's going to happen after the mating thing?"

"What happens after two humans get married? They blend their lives together."

"Are you planning to isolate her from her friends and family like you've been doing up until this point?"

"No."

Nikki makes a huffing sound. "I don't like you or any of this, but if you get my friend back in one piece I'll consider tolerating you."

"Glad to hear it."

I pick us up some food at a drive through—yes more food. I'm still hungry—then take us back into the city to the public records building. We have a whole separate building for that purpose annexed off from the courthouse.

Nikki follows me up to the door, carrying our bag of food and our drinks. "Hey, what are we doing here? It's closed."

"I've got a key and the security code." I was supposed to return it to Greg two days ago.

"And why do you have a key?"

"You ask a lot of questions. I run the top architecture firm in this city. I use the public records office a lot."

She crosses her arms over her chest while I try to use

the dim street light several yards away to find the key on my ring.

"Oh, so you're telling me architects get their own keys to government buildings?"

"No, I didn't say that. I'm friends with the City Clerk." Greg also happens to be a wolf shifter, but I don't mention this to Nikki.

"And he's allowed to just hand out keys to government buildings?"

"Probably not," I admit. Finally, I find the key and let us into the building. I punch in the security code.

Nikki flips on the lights, and I quickly turn them back off.

"What? We need to be able to see."

"We don't need that light. I don't want to draw police attention."

Nikki shrugs and follows me back to the main offices, away from the street facing windows. I flip on the lights and take our food to a long empty table. We eat and then get to work.

I turn on a couple of computers and consult the map Selene gave me, praying she isn't sending me on a wild goose chase. If she is, I'll kill her. It's almost the full moon, and if she causes my mate to die due to petty jealousy, I will end her before my own slow descent into madness can take hold.

"This will take all night," I say.

"Isn't there a database you can search? Like: houses with basements."

"It's where we'll start but we need to account for every house inside this radius and not all of them will be in the database."

"Why not?" Nikki says, swirling a french fry in her chocolate shake.

"Some of the older house plans are filed in boxes in the records room in the basement."

"And we think it's an older house?"

I shrug. "I don't know. Marcus could have had this safe house for a while."

I decide to run a quick search for basements in the area anyway. Nothing.

"Does that mean there are no basements in the database?" She's hovering over me, slurping the last remnants of her shake.

"Not necessarily. This search feature isn't the best in the world." I don't tell her that I also suspect that if Marcus bothered to put strong wards up, he probably doesn't want anything about his house to be in any kind of searchable database at all.

I pull up Google Maps and take a look at the area in question. "I think we can eliminate a third of this area," I say.

"Why?"

"It's not upscale enough. Part of this radius is a very wealthy neighborhood. Vampires tend to be extravagant, so there's no way he'll live in a middle class neighborhood, even as a temporary residence."

I set Nikki up on one of the computers and show her what we're doing. She takes half of the streets on the remaining map, and we compile a list of all the houses.

It's tedious work, but finally we've got a list of thirty-six homes, and with any luck Marcus is inside one of them. I'm grateful for the nicer neighborhoods with generous lawns. If we were dealing with anything else, we'd have a lot more houses to eliminate.

No basements are found, and fifteen of the houses aren't in the database.

"So that leaves the records room," she says.

I nod, grimly. The records room isn't the well-oiled machine that the database is, and even finding one set of house plans in this dimly lit dump is going to be nearly impossible.

The search drags on for hours.

"Hey, I found it," Nikki says.

I bolt upright. It's light outside. "What time is it? How could you let me fall asleep?"

"You were exhausted. If you're going to rescue her, you need to be rested."

She's not wrong. It's late afternoon, and Nikki seems like she'll drop at any minute. I'm grateful it's Sunday, and the office is closed for the day, or else I'd have to find a way to explain our presence to local government employees who don't take kindly to rule breakers.

I take the plans from her and confirm, that yes, this house does have a basement. We put everything back the way we found it in the records room and go back upstairs. I type the address into Google Maps, only to find a blank lot.

"Maybe the house never got built," Nikki says, her tone worried like we just did all that work for nothing.

Selene wasn't kidding about the power of his wards, if the building can't even be recorded by technology.

I shake my head. "It got built. Marcus just doesn't want to be found."

17
ROSALIE

I pace in the cell. I've eaten most of the food from the mini fridge, and now I'm just waiting for my fate. It's fifty-eight minutes until sunset. I've barely slept, and every second that ticks down, my fear climbs higher. Marcus is going to feed from me, and there won't be any bad-tasting drugs left in my blood to stop him.

What if he loses control and kills me?

What if he doesn't?

I've run the fantasy through my mind a thousand times that Cooper somehow finds and rescues me. But Marcus said he won't be able to, and even if he could, he wouldn't want me now that a vampire has tainted me.

It's so medieval. Like I'm some despoiled virgin—unwanted because I'm not pure. Some other supernatural creature's fangs have pierced my throat first, and now... what? He wouldn't want me anymore? So much for fated mates, I guess.

This fills me with so much shame. I can't even blame Cooper. I spent so much time railing against my fate that I didn't stop to consider that he's someone I would have chosen if the choice had been free. And now... this new fate turns out to be too bitter a pill.

Fifty-five minutes. I think I'm going to vomit. There's no way out of this cell. It's just a solid concrete room with a locked door and a guard on the other side. Before the sun came up, the vampire guard was switched out for a human. I heard them talking just outside the door, but I only heard enough to understand it was just a shift change.

Even if I could get out, I couldn't get away. I've tried so hard to keep it together, not to cry. Because if I start, I won't be able to stop.

I'm startled out of my fear and regret by the sound of something banging hard against the door. I take several steps back as if there's anywhere for me to run to in this cell. A second later the door swings inward. Blood drips down the metal surface. My gaze follows the blood trail down to the unconscious—or dead—human guard on the ground.

I look back up.

"Rosalie."

"Cooper." I can't even be mad that he didn't warn me about the vampires. I know I should be, but I'm just so happy to see him, and I hope with everything inside me that I'm not just dreaming all this—some last desperate fantasy before the hell really begins.

Please let this be real.

He walks into the cell and shuts the door behind him. His mating scent fills the cell, overwhelming me with a white hot blast of need. Before I can say anything, he's got me pressed against the stone wall, his mouth covering mine. I gasp against his invading tongue as his hands roam down my body. Is it really possible this is our first ever kiss?

I've had so many vivid dreams, so many sensations, and yet, this is the first time his lips have caressed over mine, the first time he's devoured me like this—like I am his only sustenance.

He pushes away from me to pull his shirt over his head. I'm hypnotized briefly by the black tribal tattoos on his chest and arms and the way his sleek muscles flex and contract as though putting on a show explicitly for my hungry gaze.

I glance at the red digital numbers counting down—fifty-two minutes—as he starts to kiss and suck on my neck. He runs his tongue over my collarbone. Wetness floods my panties in response to his increasingly possessive touch. I want to straddle his leg and ride it... I just need *anything* touching me where I need it right now. But I have to think.

I push him away, breathless. "Cooper... we need to get out of here."

He shakes his head. The look in his eyes is harder and more resolute than I've ever seen it.

"No. I don't want to be a monster with you, Rosalie, but I should have claimed you the second I had you alone in my human form. You will not be safe until this is done. And as your mate I refuse to put you in any more danger. Hate me if you must, but this is happening."

"But... does it have to be here?"

My gaze drops to his hands as he unbuttons his jeans and shoves them down. He's not wearing underwear, and I gasp as his stiff thick erection springs free from his pants.

"Yes, Rosalie." A growl escapes his chest. And I feel the bear near the surface, straining to break free with the coming moon. "We don't have time to go anywhere else. We need to get this done *now*, and get you safe."

Just the romantic words a girl longs to hear.

"But... Marcus..." I say, trying one last time to bring him back to reason.

Cooper's eyes glow golden as his mouth possessively claims mine again—an animal sound rumbling out of his chest. "He's dead until the sun sets. It's not just that he can't be in the sun. He's not even ambulatory right now. We're safe until then."

I don't ask if he killed the rest of the vampire's human servants. I know he did.

Fifty minutes.

I look back to Cooper and find pleading in his amber gaze.

"I have to do this before I shift again. The bear is crazed, and... I just need you to be safe. Please don't make me a monster. Don't fight me anymore."

My hands shake as I remove my t-shirt. I see the animal staring out at me from behind Cooper's eyes—greedily drinking me in. More and more of his humanity seems to ebb away by the moment.

He nods with approval. "Good girl."

I catch the glint of fangs in his mouth when he speaks.

I work on my jeans while he unhooks my bra. I arch up against his groping hands as he strokes and kneads my breasts. His tongue swirls over each nipple, causing them to pebble into hard points, and I can't hold back the whimper.

"Get on the mattress," he says. His voice has gone down a register, his wildness nearly overtaking him.

"Cooper..."

"*Now*, Rosalie."

I'm completely exposed as I lie on the mattress under the harsh lighting of the cell, but I don't have time to be self-conscious.

Forty-three minutes.

I expect him to just thrust into me, but he takes his time, licking and nibbling and sucking his way down my body. His fangs graze my flesh, creating a blurry line between what hurts and what feels good.

Goosebumps rise up behind his trailing tongue, and then I arch up off the mattress, a soft cry escaping my throat as he drags his wet tongue slowly over my sex.

My hands find their way into his hair as I ride his mouth. Fuck why weren't we doing this before? Only a vampire's thrall could make rappelling down a thirty story building sound like a better idea than Cooper's tongue on my pussy.

"Come for me," he growls against my sex, his low gravel voice rumbling against my flesh.

"Please, Cooper..."

"Come," he growls. "Now."

He pushes a finger inside me as his tongue works my clit, and I obey his command, babbling nonsensically, saying words that probably don't even exist as he chuckles against my mound.

"Good girl, now beg me to fuck you."

"Please... Please..." I whine.

I can't remember any other words. But this is good enough for him.

He flips me to my hands and knees, and I get a quick mental flash of my fantasies from back on the dance floor.

"I'm sorry we can't have an audience for this," he says, and I know... he *put* those images in my head that night.

I gasp when he fully seats himself inside me. I clutch

at the bare mattress, trying to find purchase, anything to grab onto as he rides me without mercy.

His cock stretches me to my limit, and I know I won't be able to go on without his dick after today. He grabs a fistful of my hair, dragging me up to him. I cry out when his fangs pierce my throat.

"Mine," he growls in my ear as he pulls away. He's still fucking me, still driving me over the edge. "Say it," he demands.

"Yours. I'm yours," the words come out a soft whimper, but he hears them.

And then he's soothing the sting away with his tongue, petting my hair as he spills inside me. I suddenly feel the energetic connection between us, like a glowing cord, and the rightness of Cooper and me seems completely inevitable—written in the stars. It seems impossible that I could have ever questioned it. I just... *know*. And I realize this is what he's felt this entire time—the absolute certainty that no other person will ever be enough.

He finally releases me and lies down. He pulls me against his body, and I let out a long sigh and stare up at the ceiling of the cell.

That was... well, okay, then. That was shifter sex. I need a moment to process all this.

We lay together panting, my heartbeat slowly returning to a normal, steady rhythm. I press my hand against the side of my throat where he bit me and sealed the wound. My fingertips trail over the puckered mark from his fangs. The vampire's bite didn't leave a mark like this.

"There will always be a scar. I marked you hard. I dare any otherworld creature to fuck around and find out again." Cooper says, a little too proudly. He gets up and gets dressed. "We've got to get to the forest."

I glance up at the timer. Thirty-two minutes until sunset. I get up and get dressed and we run together to Cooper's waiting Jeep.

The sun dips lower in the sky as we drive toward the forest breaking all reasonable speed limits.

"Will he come after us?" I ask, wondering if we're fleeing to the forest just so Cooper can shift or if there's some additional safety from the vampire there.

Cooper shakes his head. "He'll be able to smell what happened in the cell. You aren't fully human anymore, and vampires only feed from humans. He won't chase us. There's no point. And vampires hate nature."

I clench and unclench my hands in my lap. Now that the immediate threat of Marcus is gone, I have bigger fears.

"What's wrong?" he asks.

I swallow around the lump in my throat. "Nothing, just drive."

But my anxiety climbs with each passing mile.

"Goddammit Rosalie, what's wrong?"

"I'm scared. I don't know if I can handle it."

"Handle what?"

"Turning into a bear," I say softly.

"What??" He takes his eyes off the road to look at me.

"Cooper, the road!"

He swerves to get us back on course. After another minute he says, "You won't turn into a bear."

"But you bit me and said I'm not fully human."

"You aren't. You're a bear shifter's mate. There are all sorts of physiological changes going on within you, but becoming a shifter isn't one of them. Shifters are born, not made."

"But... you said when you bit me I would stop aging."

"Yes, but that doesn't mean I can turn you into a *bear*." He says this like I was completely absurd for even thinking it. "The mating bond ties you to me in a way that shares some of my life force and power with you. The effects are strongest for a human mate. So you'd still be a human... but with upgrades."

"What kind of upgrades?" The tension starts to drain out of me, but I'm still wary.

"Much longer lifespan, slower aging, robust health, quicker healing time, a lot more physical strength, more than a human male."

"But less than you?"

"Well only because I'm a shifter, and you're not."

"Oh. So, no pain every month? I mean... shifting pain, obviously as a woman I..."

"You won't have that either."

"I won't have a period?" Maybe I should have signed on to the bear shifter life mate plan earlier.

He chuckles. "No, I mean it won't hurt. All the little health problems that cause painful periods won't exist for you anymore."

I'm speechless as I let this sink in.

"See? There are benefits to being a shifter's mate." He winks at me.

"So... I could walk alone at night?" I've never been able to walk alone at night my whole life.

Cooper shrugs. "I mean, yeah. With the bond, I'd know if you were in trouble. I would still advise not going places even grown men won't go alone at night. It's not total invincibility. But it's a huge upgrade. Is that why you didn't want to be mated? Because you thought you'd have to shift?"

"One of the reasons."

"You know I'm going to mock you mercilessly for the rest of our lives about this, right?"

I punch him in the arm.

"Careful, now. You don't know your own strength anymore." But I know he's just teasing me.

We're still a few miles away from the forest when Cooper pulls to the side of the road.

"Why are we stopping?"

"I'm about to shift. I'm not going to make it. You're going to have to drive the rest of the way."

He gets out and opens the hatchback, pushing the seats down flat.

"Cooper, I can't drive with a bear in the car!"

"You'll have to. It'll be dark. I can lie down and you can cover me with those blankets." He points to some flannel blankets on the floor and doubles over in pain.

"But, bears are heavy and huge!"

"I've been in the Jeep in my bear form before. It's more space than you think, and it can handle twelve hundred pounds of cargo. I'm way less than that."

The sun disappears as the full darkness emerges, and Cooper runs into the wooded area a few yards away. I hear the horrible crunching and sounds of pain as his body breaks apart and reforms into the bear.

A wolf howls in the distance and I shiver, wondering if it's a shifter or just a regular wolf. A few minutes later Cooper emerges and climbs into the back of the Jeep. He barely fits. I cover him with the blankets and shut the door.

We've been driving a few minutes when I say,

"Cooper, can you fully understand me as a bear?" I mean I think he can. I don't know why I ask, it's not as though he can answer.

Yes, Rosalie.

I feel his thoughts push into my mind.

"Okay, I'm kind of starving," I say.

He makes a chuffing sound from the backseat that sounds suspiciously like laughter. *I'll steal us some stuff from the gas station.*

I think back, remembering the deli sandwiches he brought the first night when I ran from him. "Is that safe? What if they shoot you?"

I wouldn't die. But they won't shoot me. They made a whole Youtube channel about me. I'll show it to you when we get back home.

I'm not sure if he's serious about the Youtube channel or not.

"Cooper?"

Yeah?

"Thank you for coming for me."

It wasn't even a question. You're my mate.

His paw is stretched out on the arm rest next to me, and I put my hand on top of his paw.

Ten minutes later, we reach our destination, and I help him out of the Jeep. The night is beautiful and serene, the full moon lighting the parking lot. An owl hoots in the distance, and a small creature scampers through the leaves. The crickets begin their nightly symphony, and I hear the water flowing in a creek nearby.

I turn to Cooper and have the sudden urge to stroke his furry head. He closes his eyes and lets out a chuff as my fingers trail through his fur. It seems like a lifetime ago instead of only a month since I was lost in the woods thinking about the question of man or bear.

It's really not even a question. The answer is obvious. It was always obvious.

We share a brief psychic moment, and then I walk back into the forest with the bear.

EPILOGUE
COOPER

A *week later.*

If I could have gotten into the vampire's sleeping chamber during the day, I would have. Or maybe not. It's not right that he should die peacefully in his sleep. I considered coming for him in my bear form during the full moon and mauling him to death, but a mauling is too quick and merciful. And I want to talk… with pointy objects. I want to drag out this piece of shit's suffering for daring to touch my mate.

I thought he'd have fucked off back to Europe by now. But why should he? I didn't go after him when my brother died. Why should he think this would be any different?

It's just before sunset, and I'm sitting on top of the emptied coffin of one of his vampire guards. I took both of them out while they were sleeping. And now I sit, with a wicked-sharp dagger, waiting for Marcus to rise.

As the sun sets, the heavy vault-like bars release in a loud clang. And then the massive steel door slides open with a groan. But it's empty. There's a note on the bare marble slab. I step inside and pick it up.

The note reads, "Look behind you."

I turn to find Marcus on the outside of the vault, a sinister smile on his face. Before he can input the code to close and lock the door, I fling the dagger at him. It pierces his skin, and he collapses to the ground.

"W-what i-is this?" he asks. He's already ripped the dagger out of his throat, but it's too late.

"Dagger dipped in Vampire's Bane," I say. It won't kill him—not immediately—but it weakens him. A younger vampire would be unconscious by now.

"T-there's no s-such thing," he says, his voice going raspy.

"It's a proprietary recipe. My friend Selene whipped it up for me." For another 15k—apparently she also needs a new roof. I'm fairly certain she didn't sell it to me at market value.

I look around, wondering where he slept during the day. I guess he knew I'd come for him after all. Rowan would have killed him for taking his mate if he could have pulled himself together long enough—and if Marcus hadn't already fled the country by then.

I spot a small door, leading to another chamber. I drag the vampire back inside. It's a windowless dungeon, a good secondary resting place for a vampire—not quite as secure as the vault for a being that falls completely dead each day—but safe enough in a pinch.

This room isn't mostly empty like the cell I found

Rosalie in, no this one is meant for... playing. I push down the bile rising in my throat at the thought of the things he would have done to her in here if I hadn't gotten to her in time.

There is all manner of bondage and sex furniture, sex toys, whips and chains, as well as weapons hanging on the wall... swords, axes, and knives. The space seems to serve as a play room, a torture dungeon, and general weapons storage.

I drag Marcus over to a set of chains and secure him. He seems even weaker, and I'm afraid he'll nod off. Fuck. I want him to be fully aware as I take him apart piece by piece. Slowly. I want to drag this out until I am satisfied.

I pull the phone from my pocket and call Selene.

"Coven Mart, how may I help you?"

"He's about to go unconscious on me. How long until this wears off?"

"Oh. I might have used a little too much belladonna."

"How long?"

I can practically hear her shrug over the phone.

"I mean, possibly twenty years. Give or take."

"Selene..."

"I'm kidding. Throw some water on him and smack him around a little. Just keep him awake for a few minutes and it should wear off. Vampires bounce back."

I growl and hang up the phone. I run upstairs, grab a glass, and pour some cold water from the faucet. Then I go back down to splash it in the vampire's face.

He spits and splutters when the water hits him. I smack him a few times. His vision finally seems to clear, and his fangs descend.

"I'll kill you," he says.

"When you make your impossible escape from shackles you're too drugged to break out of?"

A dagger, my dagger, flies past my head and embeds into the wall.

"No, when my new human servants release me."

I turn to see five burly guys piling into the dungeon. They look like members of a biker gang and probably were before Marcus recruited them and pressed them into his service.

I am so angry right now that I can't fulfill my original plan, but Rosalie comes first, and if I get myself killed... it would be too cruel to her.

"Fuck you for making me do this quick," I snarl.

I grab a sword off the wall and lop off the vampire's head. The head rolls on the floor at my feet, turning gray right in front of me. As his body begins to disintegrate I see the ghost of a smile on his face like even in death he thinks he won a round.

I look back up to the humans who seem spooked—now freed from the vampire's thrall—and confused about what they're even doing down here. I don't bother explaining what they just witnessed. They'd refuse to believe it anyway.

When I get back to the penthouse, I find Rosalie on the rooftop, painting. We've set up a makeshift open-air workspace for her until I can design and build a properly ventilated and temperature-controlled studio up here. Right now there's a steel closet she can store everything in when she's not working to protect all her stuff from the weather.

We've discussed a large structure with huge glass windows so she gets all the angles of the sun without obstruction.

A couple of days ago the gallery she exhibited at called. They're getting calls and emails requesting more of her work. She's been invited to do a solo show at the city's largest art museum which I designed the renovation for. A major fine art review publication wants to feature her show in a story that's going to combine art with the public interest angle of wildlife conservation.

Rosalie stands out in the clear sunny day, wearing a white smock covered in paint. Her hair is swept into a messy updo. I slip behind her and pull her back against my chest. I smell her citrus and honey scent and run my tongue over the puckered scar of my mating mark.

She shivers and sighs contentedly against me. "Where'd you go?"

"I just had an errand to run. Are you near a stopping point?"

She pulls out of my arms and steps back to take a look at her newest painting. It's another bear and woman. It's a large scale piece. One half of the painting is a dark, gritty dirty city and the other side is the beauty, splendor, and magic of the forest. The bear is leading the woman from the city back into nature.

I want to hang it in our penthouse, but I know she needs work to sell, so I keep this feeling to myself. Anyway, I have the first one in this series.

She sighs, "I could probably take a break."

"Good. Get your cute ass into my bed." I smack said cute ass, and she lets out a shriek of laughter as she races back inside, and I spend the rest of the day in bed reminding her of all the perks of being mine.

BONUS EPILOGUE
ROSALIE

Ten years later.

It's the final night of the full moon. I'm snuggled up with Cooper in our den, his furry bear arm holding me close as he snores softly behind me. Bear snores are somehow a thousand times more endearing than human, and he doesn't snore in his human form, so I'll look past it.

But I can't sleep, mostly because our two cubs are grabbing their feet and rolling all around the den, making little chuffing noises. It's both distracting and adorable. Yes, they're twins, and no, they weren't born as bears. Rose and Rowan were born human—or human looking, anyway. Their first shift happened three months ago, and I was so worried for them, but they handled it well. They *love* being bears.

I just want to boop their cute little baby bear noses.

I still can't get over how much a bear cub's cry sounds like a baby's cry. Since the first time I heard it, I've learned it's so uncanny that mother bears sometimes mistake human baby cries for their own cubs. This might explain why there seem to be so many stories of small children lost in the woods and protected by bears. I fully believe these stories—and I don't think it's always a shifter.

My family and friends obviously don't know about Cooper and the cubs. The bear thing, I mean. They know we had a whirlwind romance and got married—mostly so we wouldn't have to hear about *why* we weren't married when we were so clearly perfect for each other. Of course they know we have twins, and thankfully the babies gestated the normal human length of time so there were no uncomfortable questions. I had to see a special shifter baby doctor for obvious reasons. Apparently there are some strange things that would look like abnormalities during human development but are just fine for a bear shifter.

But the people in my life don't know and can't know anything beyond that. Cooper and I got into a heated argument over whether or not he should get Selene to do a forgetting spell on Nikki in order to keep his secret. But in the end, Nikki stayed in the loop, mainly because I told Cooper he'd just be wasting all his money getting his ex to do forgetting spells because I was just going to keep telling Nikki the truth. I have to have someone to talk to about all this, after all.

I'm not exactly sure how we're going to explain the fact that we don't seem to age to my family. But I'm sure there's a plan in place for handling this. Maybe a glamour to cause us to "appear to age"? I don't know what the limitations of magic are but I'm sure there's a strategy—otherwise the whole human world would know about the other world. Shifter and human matings are quite common after all.

Cooper calls Rose and Rowan our miracle cubs because he really thought it would take us a hundred years to have them, if we had any at all. We're looking into some stronger birth control options to keep this from happening again—at least for a while. Once the cubs are grown we'd like a good hundred years to ourselves before parenting again.

Despite how busy the last several years have been, we've had a lot of help from other shifters in the larger community—including a full time nanny. I've managed to create a shocking amount of art in this time. I'm now what you would call "Artist famous". Not quite as well known as Banksy or Picasso, but I'm definitely moving in the upper echelons of the contemporary art world. Just last week I had a painting sell at auction for fifty-two thousand dollars. It was part of my expanded woman and bear series, which shows no signs of slowing in popularity.

I sigh. I'm never going to get back to sleep with the cubs playing. I shimmy out from under Cooper's paw and get dressed in some jeans and a T-shirt. I pull on hiking boots and put my hair up in a ponytail.

"Hey," I whisper to the cubs, "let's go for a walk."

They bounce along behind me as I guide us outside into the warm summer night. The full moon lights the path, though I don't really need it. I got some vision upgrades when Cooper bit me. It took me a few weeks after the mating was complete to realize I could see in the dark. It's probably my favorite upgrade. I feel like a cat. Having what I would consider "superpowers" combined with night vision has made being out by myself at night much less scary. I have one hundred percent confidence that I could take a creepy stranger in the woods if such an unfortunate encounter ever happened again.

Can we go swimming, mama? Rose thinks at me.

Yeah! Rowan's little mind joins her. *I'm gonna catch a fish.*

Ordinarily, I would say no. It's two o'clock in the morning. But swimming makes you sleepy, and if I want to get back to sleep tonight, this is the fastest way to make that happen.

The cubs have been splashing around in the lake for about fifteen minutes when I hear a much louder chuffing sound. I turn to find Cooper.

"You can't sleep either?" I ask when he sits down on a rock beside me.

My brain is trying to design a building, so no.

"Do you know what sounds really good right now?"

What?

"One of those deli sandwiches from the gas station." They're bad-good. "They're open all night," I say, batting my eyelashes and pouting.

Cooper sighs. *You're lucky you're so cute. Tomorrow night when I get my human form back, I'm not letting you out of my bed. Possibly for days.*

"Are you telling me the sandwich is going to cost me?"

You have no idea.

"I have some idea."

He nuzzles my neck over the mating mark scar, then gets up to go get sandwiches.

"I love you," I say sweetly.

You're just using me for my hunting prowess.

I laugh. I watch my mate disappear into the forest then turn back to our cubs splashing in the water.

Look! I got a fish! Rowan thinks at me.

"Good job, buddy!"

I stare up at the moon. Already its fullness is fading. Cooper will be back to human form in less than six hours. He's crazy if he thinks I'm waiting all the way until tomorrow night to *pay for my deli sandwich*. I pull out my phone, forgetting about the bad reception out here. But... what do you know? I get bars by the lake. That would have been useful knowledge to have that first night when I was trying to escape.

I get on the internet and book a nice hotel room in the city. I fully intend to kidnap Cooper from work tomorrow. And I don't plan to let him out of *my* bed for a very long time.

BEHIND THE SCENES WITH KITTY

Hello my little bag of trail mix,

This story was inspired directly out of the men of the internet losing their goddamned minds over the fact that the vast vast majority of women are less afraid of encountering a bear in the woods than a man. There were a lot of TikToks and a lot of Youtubes and honestly it was pretty epic. I took a two week break from Youtube to finish up my Game Maker re-release and bonus epilogue and when I returned the Bear vs. Man discussion was still blazing strong.

People had started #TeamBear, and the discussion of "This is why we'd pick the bear" started showing up in all sorts of contexts and discussions around men.

So when this book idea showed up, it just felt timely.

A whole bunch of women came together to talk about why they felt this way, and a whole bunch of men got all up in their ego and feelings and decided women are just hysterical and irrational and don't understand bears are dangerous. Or that we "hate men" or that "most men are good and we're just overreacting." etc. The thing is... given the historical centuries of enslavement and no rights, if women DID hate men, it would be warranted for that treatment. Fifty to a hundred years of rights does not override millennia of suffering, particularly when certain parts of the world are still awful for women, the west is becoming more awful for women, and men are rising up in backlash screaming that "feminism has gone too far" because they feel so entitled to sex and our unpaid domestic labor.

I personally think women are far too forgiving. And if we collectively were far less forgiving, we'd be living in a matriarchy right now.

Anyway, back to the actual book. I was supposed to be starting a different book but I woke up with this scene in my head where Cooper, in bear form, rescues Rosalie from an attacker. And so I thought... you know I'll just write a little smutty short story. (Because who doesn't get almost attacked in the woods and then instantly proceed to fall into the arms of their rescuer for some hot, sweaty sex?) This short story quickly expanded into a novella.

The title came quickly, and my artist had a great idea with the claw marks and the man chest because... I don't care what anybody says, people love a man chest cover. Maybe not for riding on the subway with a paperback book but... for an e-reader? Yes.

Early in my writing career I used to HATE man chest covers. But I have grown to appreciate them. I think it's just that the "Fabio look" isn't my type. I like guys who look more like the guy on the cover of Berserker or The Game Maker (both the new and the old cover.) I like the muscles that hide well under a suit and are sleek outside of it. Not the overly bulky "alpha bro" gym rat look.

The painting of the woman and the bear in the story is actually a description of a painting that I own. I've had it for a long time, and it holds personal spiritual meaning to me. But I think it's funny that now if people come to my house and see it, they'll wonder if it's some kind of political statement. (It isn't.)

I've been a collector of original art for about 7 years now. I really just like having art that nobody else has. And there is a thrill to finding a new piece or discovering an artist whose work really speaks to me. And while technically, the artist could make and sell a print, it's still not the same. A painting carries a kind of "life" in it that a print does not. I do have a few prints, but that's mostly on walls where there's just too much direct sunlight, where I wouldn't want to put an original piece because of sun damage.

A lot of people stay away from art collecting because they think it's prohibitively expensive, but unknown artists doing smaller art pieces... it's much more affordable than you would think. And there's a lot of great original art on places like Etsy. Small local galleries and museum gift shops are also great places to look. I collect a wide range of things: pastels, oils, watercolors, acrylics. Animals, still lifes, some landscapes, a little bit of abstract. I'm not a huge fan of abstract art, but there is some that looks amazing. I want my whole house to basically look like an art museum.

I think this is my third book that has a character who is an artist. Two others are The Con Artist and Berserker—though in Berserker it's mentioned in passing.

But I digress. We are getting super off topic here.

Mating Season is a bit of a captive story and has some dark elements but I'm not sure I'd call it "dark" in the way many of my other books are... maybe "light dark PNR". I've always wanted to write a bear shifter but just never got around to it, but thanks to the freak out on the internet about #TeamBear, I finally got to write one.

This one also has some humor kind of on the level of Berserker. So if you're new to my work or haven't read Berserker and enjoyed Mating Season, then you should check out Berserker next!

Be sure to sign up for my newsletter at kittythomas.com for all the things and to get a free ebook.

Thanks so much for reading and supporting my work,

Kitty ^.^

OTHER BOOKS BY KITTY THOMAS

If you enjoyed MATING SEASON, you'll also love BERSERKER:

If you'd like more paranormal but on the darker side with vampires, I recommend you check out BLOOD MATE next: